River Dream

A Novel

Beverly,

May all your River
Dreams come true.

D W Davis

Published by River Sailor Literary
River Sailor Literary
Post Office Box 189
Pikeville, North Carolina 27863-0189, USA

ISBN: 0983355614
ISBN-13: 9780983355618

Acknowledgements

To my lovely wife, Karen, and our sons, Alex and Zack, whose encouragement and enthusiasm kept me going, and kept me believing in my own river dreams.
To the sailing staff at Camp Don-Lee for giving me the chance to learn that, despite waiting so long to find out, sailing can take me away to where I want to be. The time I spent with the wind and water helped launch the ideas that became River Dream.
To my co-workers: Lovely, Stacey, and Michelle, for reading my rough drafts, and encouraging me to keep going.
To two very special young adult readers, Jamilynne and Donald: They took a chance, read the draft, and convinced me I had a book here their peers would want to read.
And especially to my friend and editor, Jeanie Sherman, without whose encouragement, advice, and support I could never have made it from draft to published work. Thank you all so much for helping make my River Dream come true.

Table of Contents

One 1

Two 5

Three 13

Four 23

Five 29

Six 35

Seven 41

Eight 57

Nine.. 67

Ten 77

Eleven 89

Twelve 93

Thirteen.. 99

Fourteen 109

Fifteen 115

Sixteen 119

Seventeen 129

Eighteen... 141

Nineteen 147

Twenty 153

Twenty-one.. 159

Twenty-two.. 165

Twenty-three 171

Twenty-four 173

Twenty-five 177

Twenty-six.. 189

Twenty-seven.. 191

Twenty-eight 199

Twenty-nine 205

Thirty.. 219

One

May 1976

The rain came down so hard we could hardly hear the bells on the pinball machine. I was so close to winning a free play I could taste it, but then the ball took a weird bounce off the last bumper and drained neatly between the flippers. I grimaced. Rhiannon laughed.

"Looks like no free game for you this time, Mike."

I slapped the sides of the machine in frustration and moved back to make room for her to play. A clap of thunder drowned out everything for a moment, and we looked towards the doors leading out to the pier. On a night like that nobody went fishing. We pretty much had the pier house to ourselves.

Rhiannon was my best friend. We'd known each other nearly all our lives. On top of that, I was in love with her as only a ninth grade boy could be. Rhiannon, the red-haired, green-eyed object of my affection did not return the feeling with the same intensity.

Calling Rhiannon's hair red may have been overstating the case. It was more auburn than red, as she would remind me whenever I commented on her red-headed temper. Her eyes, though, were definitely green, a beautiful emerald green. When she laughed, like she did at me that night, they seemed to sparkle. If she was angry, they were as cold and hard as the stone whose color they shared.

Rhiannon was nearly as tall as I was, and I was already five-ten by the end of ninth grade. She'd been a cheerleader all through junior high and taken some gymnastics when she was younger, but didn't have the thin build of your typical gymnast. She did look great in a bikini though.

We were hanging out together by the pinball machine like we did almost every night. Rhiannon's family owned the pier. My family lived a short way across South Lumina Avenue on the sound side of the island.

We'd gotten into a routine in fourth grade where I'd carry my books up to the pier after supper so Rhiannon and I could do our homework together in the snack bar. Now, ninth grade was almost over.

I couldn't remember a time when I hadn't known Rhiannon. Almost from birth we were spending time together. My mother would walk me over to the pier in my stroller and put me in the playpen while she visited Rhiannon's mom, Cassie.

When I was a little older my grandfather, who lived with us, would bring me with him to the pier and leave me to play with Rhiannon while he fished or traded fish stories with her father, Lindsey. Lindsey Angevin had been Uncle Lind to me since I was a toddler. By first grade I was walking up to the pier by myself. You could pretty much say Rhiannon and I grew up on that pier together.

The summer between sixth and seventh grade I began to notice Rhiannon wasn't just another kid to hang out with. I mean I always knew she was a girl, but I began to notice she was kind of cute. It's also when I began falling in love with her. When I'd told her this, she'd wrinkled her nose at me and said, "Oh gross, Michael, you're not supposed to say that."

We were out on the pier trying to catch spot when I told her. It was near dusk and the fish hadn't started biting, so I decided it was a good time to announce my feelings. Perhaps I was wrong.

"Why not?" I asked perplexed, "I do think you're cute."

"I am not," Rhiannon protested, turning her face away and rolling her eyes. "Stop saying that."

I leaned closer to her on the bench. "You are too," I insisted. "I think I love you. Can I be your boyfriend?"

Rhiannon shook her head fiercely and started reeling in her line. "No way Mike, I'm too young for a boyfriend. Besides, you're my real friend; you can't be my boyfriend."

I didn't understand her logic. I checked my line - nothing. My attention went back to Rhiannon. "Why can't I be your boyfriend?"

She looked at me like the answer was so obvious I shouldn't have to ask. Letting out a frustrated sigh, she cast her line back out. "You can't be my boyfriend because you're my best friend. You can't be both, that's just the rules."

Now it was my turn to be frustrated. "I've never heard of those rules."

"Well, I don't want to talk about it anymore," Rhiannon said with a toss of her head.

That pretty much ended the conversation because once Rhiannon made up her mind, her mind was made up. I figured if I waited long enough, she would relent. That's why, on our bus ride home from Noble Junior High School one day early on in seventh grade, I asked her to our first junior high school dance.

"Michael, I already told you, we can't be boyfriend and girl-friend," Rhiannon reminded me, turning to look out the bus window.

Shifting in my seat to face her more squarely, I said, "I'm not asking you to be my girlfriend," hoping to win on a technicality. "I'm just asking you to the dance."

She continued to look out the window. "Michael, you only ask a girl to the dance if you want her to be your girlfriend. It's like asking her on a date. We can't go on a date because we're best friends. Best friends don't date." Finally turning to look at me, she punctuated it with, "That's just the rules."

I don't know where she kept getting those rules from but it was pretty clear she wasn't going to the dance with me. Employing logic that made sense only to a pubescent boy, I decided to ask another girl in our seventh grade class. My thinking was that somehow it would make Rhiannon wish she'd gone with me. Besides, Elisabeth Bosworth was kind of cute, rather petite, with short brown hair and soft brown eyes, and we were good friends. I didn't tell her Rhiannon had already turned me down.

Beth looked genuinely disappointed as she told me, "Gee Mike, I already told Greg Puckett I'd go with him. He asked me yesterday. I wish you'd asked me sooner. I'd have liked to go with you." Suddenly her face brightened as if she'd had a wonderful idea. "Hey, why don't you ask Rhiannon?" I found that rather ironic.

Two

The night of the dance was an adventure for all of us. It was the first junior high school dance any of us had been to. Though we weren't technically going to the dance together, Rhiannon and I both rode to the dance with her father. My father was going to pick us up when it was over.

Our little group of friends wound up sitting with a couple of kids who were new to the school. The two of them had each come alone and wound up at the same table because neither of them really knew anyone else there. Having seen them around school and knowing they were new, I decided to barge in on them and introduce us all.

"Hi," I said, "can we join you?"

The new guy looked at the girl as if to ask if she minded. She shrugged and smiled.

"Sure, there's plenty of room," he said. "I'm Eric, and this is Juliet."

Eric's medium brown hair reached just past his ears, and his brown eyes were framed by gold-rimmed glasses. He was on the thin side. I recalled from seeing him around school that he wasn't very tall.

Juliet's eyes were a lighter brown, and seemed to be flaked with gold. Her hair might have been dark blond or light brown, depending on how much time she spent in the sun. She was as tall as Rhiannon, maybe a little taller, with a medium build.

"I'm Mike, and these're my friends Rhiannon and Beth." I gestured at Beth's date with a nod of my head. "He's Beth's friend Greg."

Eric gave me an odd look when I introduced Greg that way. I suppose it was odd, but Greg was Beth's friend; I never really liked him. About then my friend Hans walked up with his date, April.

Hans was born in Stuttgart. His parents emigrated from Germany to the United States when he was barely a year old. In seventh grade Hans was one inch taller than I was and very proud of it. He wore his dark hair long and shaggy. It reached his shoulders. Hans' eyes were such a dark brown they looked almost black.

Rhiannon and I had known Hans since we were all about three. His mother became an avid pier fisherman after his father started working second shift. Hans would come with her and wound up spending more time playing with me and Rhiannon than fishing with her. Our parents sometimes referred to us collectively as the three mulleteers, a play on Dumas' famous trio.

"Guys, meet Eric and his girlfriend Juliet." When I introduced them Eric started to tell me Juliet wasn't his girlfriend, but the look on her face stopped him. He gave her what I thought was a look asking 'is that okay with you?' and she responded with a smile and a slight nod.

"Hi, everyone," Eric said as he and Juliet moved their chairs closer together to make room for us all.

Rhiannon took the seat next to Juliet. "You guys're new around here, aren't you?" she asked before looking at me with something just short of a scowl and motioning to the chair next to hers.

Feeling a bit awkward at being noticed as a stranger, Juliet replied, "I just moved here this summer. Eric got here last spring."

"Oh," Rhiannon commented, "didya know each other where you lived before?" She was not the least bit shy about quizzing our new friends.

"Actually," Eric took up the narration and told her, "Juliet's from Atlanta and I'm from Norfolk. We met here at school."

I sat down next to Rhiannon after only a moment's hesitation. Considering we weren't technically there together, she seemed intent on keeping me close by. Addressing Eric and Juliet, I said, "That's cool. Rhiannon and I are both from around here. We live down at the beach, practically across the street from each other."

"Juliet, I think we have Language Arts together," Beth said as she took the chair to my left, earning her a curious look from Rhiannon.

"Yes, Mrs. Ballentine's class," Juliet said, glad to have found common ground. "Don't you think she's a great teacher?"

"I like her," said Rhiannon, who was also in their class.

The girls started talking about teachers they had, which ones were better, and their favorite subjects. Eric turned to me and asked how long Rhiannon and I had been going out.

Rhiannon's head snapped around. "Oh, we're not going out," she informed him. "He's my best friend, but we're not boyfriend and girlfriend."

Her words pained me a little, but I managed a smile. "There you have it, Eric. Rhiannon has a rule about not dating her best friend, me."

Eric managed a confused smile before moving on to Greg. "Greg, how about you and Beth?"

"This is our first date," Greg answered distractedly. From the look on his face I got the impression Greg didn't like the way Beth had chosen to sit next to me.

Eric looked at Hans and Hans told him, "April and I have known each other since fourth grade. Sometimes she is my girlfriend," he explained with emphasis on the is, "and sometimes not. Lucky for me today she is."

"And if you're lucky I still will be tomorrow," April offered.

Hans laughed and asked her to dance. I took the opportunity to ask Rhiannon to dance. We might not be dating, but she would always dance with me when I asked. Eric led Juliet to the dance floor as well. When the song ended, we made our way back to the table where Greg and Beth had remained during the song.

"So, Juliet, how tall are you anyway?" Greg asked when we sat back down. Beth gave him a sharp look, but Juliet handled it with aplomb.

"I get that all the time," she said to Beth before turning an icy smile on Greg. "How tall do you think I am?"

Greg noticed the way the rest of us were looking at him. "Hey, I was just asking. She's very tall."

"I think you owe her an apology," I said. The guy just got on my nerves.

"It's all right, Mike," Juliet said. "I'm used to it. I'm five feet six inches tall, Greg. How short are you?"

I chuckled. Greg was somewhat short for his age. Maybe that's why Beth liked him, being rather petite herself. Hans shot me a warning glance and motioned with his head to Beth. Looking at her I could tell she didn't like where the conversation was headed.

"Greg," Beth suggested, "why don't we go get a drink?" Greg looked like he was about to say something stupid, but Beth was already out of her seat and taking hold of his arm. Sensibly he rose and accompanied her. They chose to sit at a different table, with his friends, afterward.

"What's with him?" Eric asked no one in particular.

I probably should have kept my mouth shut. Instead I said, "Puckett's always been a jerk."

"You don't like him because he asked Beth to the dance before you did," Rhiannon accused me.

"That's not true. I've never liked him. He's always been such an…"

"Watch your language, Michael," Rhiannon warned me.

I looked at her and realized she was right.

"Why let him spoil the dance for the rest of us?"

Taking Rhiannon by the hand, I pulled her out onto the dance floor. As we danced I said to Rhiannon, "You know, if you'd just said you'd go to the dance with me, I wouldn't even have asked Beth."

"Michael," Rhiannon replied patiently, "I've explained this to you. We're best friends. Best friends don't date. Dating destroys friendships."

"I know," I said resignedly, "it's one of your rules. But Rhiannon, your dad brought us here, my dad is picking us up, we sit together and we dance together. How is this not a date?"

"You're not going to get a good night kiss," Rhiannon said. She tried to soften it with a smile. "You're my best friend, Michael. We're not going to screw that up."

I looked over at Eric and Juliet. His head was on her shoulder. I wondered if being practically strangers made it easier to be boyfriend and girlfriend. Maybe someday I would find out. Or maybe not. Rhiannon might not be willing to admit it, but I had a feeling someday she would realize she was my Juliet.

"It's not going to happen, Michael," Rhiannon whispered with a knowing smile. It's as if she read my mind.

The pattern was set. Each dance for the next three years I would ask Rhiannon and she would say no. We'd wind up riding together anyway, but Rhiannon would remind me that didn't make it a date. Nor did the fact that we always sat at the same table and danced to most of the songs make it a date. Even the dirty looks Rhiannon gave me when I danced with other girls, looks she wouldn't admit to, couldn't cause her to bend her rule.

Eric and Juliet made lots of new friends, and we didn't really hang out with them much after that first dance. Beth went to every dance with Greg. April usually went with Hans, but once in a while she'd get mad at him and go with someone else. I found myself wondering if Hans ever asked Rhiannon out, so one day I asked him point blank.

He looked surprised I would even ask. "Why would I? She's your girlfriend."

"Really, did she tell you that?"

"No, I just assumed she was," Hans shrugged and said. "I mean, I know she says she isn't but, Michael, it sure seems to me like she is.

"If she is, it's news to me. Every time I ask her out she says no."

"I don't understand. You love her, yes? You sit together at lunch. You dance at the dances. You see her every day at the pier. The two of you sail together whenever you can. Now you tell me you two are not a couple. What are you then?"

He wasn't any more confused than I was. "According to Rhiannon, we're best friends, and best friends can't date. It's the rules."

"What rules?" Hans asked.

"Darned if I know," I confessed.

Hans was right when he said Rhiannon and I did everything together: fishing, sailing, hanging out at the beach. We sat next to each other at lunch and danced at the school dances. I suppose friends do those things, except maybe the last one. After all, Hans and I did all those things together too, except the dancing part. More to the point, I hadn't fallen in love with Hans.

Hans looked at me with a sympathetic smile. "Give it time, Michael. She'll see you're the one for her."

Three

Standing at the end of the Camp Riversail dock on a clear day, you can see for miles down the Neuse River toward Pamlico Sound. Two miles upstream the river bends sharply around Shark Tooth Point and narrows as it approaches New Bern and its confluence with the Trent River. The Neuse doesn't really flow between New Bern and the Sound; it's more a tidal basin of brackish water tinted the color of iced tea by the leaves washed in as it meanders through the North Carolina Coastal Plain from its headwaters in the Piedmont near Raleigh.

I was eight when I went away to Camp Riversail for the first time. Sailing had always been part of my life but that summer at camp raised my love of it to a whole new level. Over my years at camp I learned to do just about everything a guy can do on or in the water. Camp also taught me a lot about the river, its environment and its inhabitants. It was at Camp I got the idea for River Dream, my home on the river.

The summer after seventh grade ended I headed off to Camp Riversail again. Rhiannon seemed sad to see me go, especially after learning I would be there for three weeks, my longest stint yet. She was still stubbornly sticking to her rules, and I was still stubbornly hoping she'd come around.

It was that summer I met a special girl, Christy Ann. Christy Ann Cunningham was from Hickory, North Carolina. She was a pretty girl with dark brown hair and warm brown eyes that looked out through a pair of thin gold-framed glasses. Christy Ann was my age but a good bit shorter than me; her head only came up to my shoulder. She had a really cute, if slightly crooked, smile.

Christy Ann had never been to Camp Riversail before. She'd always gone to camp up in the mountains but, that year, convinced her parents to let her try the coast. Christy Ann knew very little about boats and even less about sailing. I took it upon myself to help her learn. After all, I'd been sailing since I could walk.

Our first night Christy Ann sat with me at the campfire. "Is it always this hot around here?" she asked with a sigh.

"Only during summer," I explained as I skewered a marshmallow on a stick and handed it to her. "Winters can get pretty cold, on and off."

She held the stick out toward the fire but not close enough to actually cook the marshmallow. "I don't think it ever gets this hot around Hickory. Have you ever been to Hickory, Mikey?"

Christy Ann insisted on calling me Mikey. I'd never let anyone call me Mikey, not at Camp, not at home, not before then, and not since. For some reason though, it never bothered me when Christy Ann called me Mikey.

"I've been through there on my way to the mountains. We drive out to Asheville once in a while." Seeing how far her marshmallow was from the heat, I took her hand and gently guided it closer to the fire. "I spend most of my summer here at Camp." Sure, it was a slight exaggeration, but I thought it would impress her.

Christy Ann smiled shyly when I touched her hand and glanced at me out of the corner of her eye. Looking back into the camp fire she asked, "How long you been coming here to Camp?"

Settling back against the log as I held my own marshmallow out to the fire, I said as casually as I could, "This is my sixth summer."

Her eyes widened. "Wow, you've been coming since you were just a little kid then."

I shrugged and nodded, trying to act like it was no big deal.

"You must know a lot about sailboats and sailing." Her marshmallow had barely started to brown, but she took it from the fire and popped it into her mouth.

"Yeah, I guess you could say that."

"Maybe you can help me learn," Christy Ann suggested while licking the marshmallow off her lips. "I don't know anything about them."

I was so captivated watching Christy Ann eat her marshmallow I didn't notice mine catch fire. "I'd like to," I said as I put out the burning end of my stick in the sand. "I love helping people learn to sail."

Rising early the next morning, I walked out to the end of the dock to watch the sunrise. No wind disturbed the waters of the Neuse as I stood against the rail and watched the first rays of the sun appear over the far bank. That would change as the sun continued its climb and the air warmed. The quiet calm of dawn would soon give way to the sound of sails snapping in the breeze.

Those of us with more experience were paired with a novice sailor. Christy Ann asked Rachel, the lead girls' counselor, if she could be paired with me, and Rachel said it would be all right. We sailed Aqua Finns those first couple of days, getting the basics down for the new kids, and getting us old hands back in shape.

The Aqua Finn, at about fourteen feet and with only one sail, is an easy boat for the beginning sailor to learn on. It resembles a large surfboard with a shallow cockpit and can be sailed by one, two, or if they're small, three people. With its single sail, an Aqua Finn needs only one line, which sailors call a sheet, and the tiller.

Before Christy Ann and I pushed off for the first time, Rachel took me aside. "Michael," Rachel said in a serious tone, "I want you to be extra careful with Christy Ann."

"Rachel, I'm always careful," I assured her with a cocky grin. Rachel knew what kind of sailor I was. We'd sailed together plenty of times.

"Extra careful, Michael," Rachel emphasized. Her expression told me this was important to her.

Somewhat puzzled I asked, "Why extra careful?"

"Just do it, Michael, because I asked you to, please," Rachel implored me, concern showing clearly in her eyes.

"All right," I promised solemnly, "I'll be extra careful." I looked over at Christy Ann and wondered what Rachel was so worked up about. Christy Ann was waiting on the sand by our boat, adjusting her life jacket to a more comfortable fit. Shrugging to myself, I decided not to ask about it; I didn't want to embarrass her.

We had a great day on the water. Christy Ann learned quickly and was tacking and jibing in no time. I think she enjoyed the capsize drills more than anything else. At the nightly campfire we talked about nothing but sailing.

Those first couple days we didn't stray far from camp. We practiced with the Aqua Finns until the counselors were confident we could handle them. Then it was time for our first excursion, a day trip around Shark's Tooth Point up to Minnesott Beach, about two miles upriver toward New Bern. Two miles might not sound far, but we had to beat to weather getting there, which was very tiring.

Beating to weather is a sailor's way of saying we sailed upwind. Christy Ann got pretty worn out about half-way there, so I gave her a break and single-hand sailed the Aqua Finn the rest of the way.

"I'm sorry I got so pooped out," Christy Ann apologized as we approached the beach.

"Don't worry about it, Christy Ann," I said as I pulled up the dagger board. The dagger board was a removable board that acted as a keel. Prepared to beach the boat, I sat back and smiled at her. "Sailing is a lot more work than people think."

Christy Ann smiled back. "It doesn't look like work when I watch you doing it."

"I've been sailing most of my life," I reminded her. "It's almost second nature to me."

"Too bad I'll never get to be good at it."

"Sure you will. All it takes is time and practice."

"I wish I had the time," Christy Ann said sadly. I thought she meant living way out in Hickory she wouldn't get to go sailing very often.

When we got to the beach Rachel came over to check on us. "How are you doing, Christy Ann?"

"I'm kind of tired," Christy Ann said. "I wasn't much help to Mikey sailing the boat today."

"Don't you worry, Michael can handle the boat," Rachel told her cheerfully, but I could see the concern on the counselor's face. "Are you up to sailing back after lunch, or should I call for a ride?"

Christy Ann didn't like the idea of riding back. "If Mikey doesn't mind doing most of the work, I can sail back."

"I don't think Mikey will mind," Rachel said sweetly, emphasizing the Mikey.

"You're not allowed to call me Mikey," I somewhat rudely informed Rachel.

"You don't seem to mind Christy Ann calling you that," Rachel responded with what might have been a hint of jealousy.

"She's the only one allowed to call me that."

"Fine, Michael, you don't mind sailing Christy Ann back, do you?"

"Christy Ann and I'll do just fine sailing our boat back together. We're crew mates."

"Just make sure you take good care of her," Rachel warned me before walking off to check on the other sailors. As she did, Bart, my cabin counselor, came over to talk to me. "Mike, what'd you say to tick Rachel off?"

"He didn't say anything," Christy Ann said. "Rachel was being kind of a pain in the neck." Bart and I both looked at Christy Ann in surprise. "What, can't I stick up for my crew mate?"

Bart laughed. "Sure you can," he said. "That's what good crew mates do." He told us to enjoy our lunch and went off to find his own.

Moving close beside me as I secured the boat on the beach, Christy Ann said, "Thank you, Mikey."

Lifting the cooler containing our lunch from the cockpit, I asked, "For what?"

"For not letting Rachel make me ride back to camp instead of sail."

"I wasn't going to let you miss the fun," I said. "We'll be sailing back before the wind. It'll be a blast."

Christy Ann smiled and handed me my ham-and-cheese sandwich. We finished our lunch in silence, then got ready for the return trip back around the point to camp. On the return we had the wind to our backs a good bit of the way and skimmed across the water. Some of the other boats capsized, but not ours. We could have been the first ones back, but I looped out wide and came in on a beam reach. I don't think Rachel was too happy about it. Christy Ann loved it.

At campfire Rachel took me aside. "Michael, that was a fool stunt you pulled today. I told you to be careful with Christy Ann."

Irked by her attitude I shot back, "I was careful. Just because you couldn't have made that move doesn't mean it wasn't safe for me to."

Rachel put her hands on her hips and gave me a hard look. "What do you mean?"

"I think you know what I mean."

"Are you trying to say you're a better sailor than I am?"

"I don't think that's open to debate."

Rachel knew I was the better sailor but hated having me point it out to her.

"Well, tomorrow when we move to the Scotts I'm putting Christy Ann on a different boat," she threatened.

I couldn't reign in my sarcasm. "Not your boat, I hope."

"Why not my boat?" Rachel demanded to know.

"You want to keep her safe, don't you?" I chided her. "Then don't put her on your boat."

"You're a jerk, Michael," Rachel said, close to tears.

I might have felt a twinge of guilt, or maybe not.

"That may be, but I like Christy Ann and I wouldn't let anything hurt her. Try putting her on another boat and see what happens."

"She'll be on your boat, Mike," Bart said as he walked over to us. "Rachel, I don't know what your problem is with Mike, but it's clearly affecting your ability to do your job."

"He's an arrogant little jerk is the problem," Rachel sniffed.

"Well," Bart said, "you seem to be the only one who brings out that side of his personality. Maybe I need to talk to Mr. Cooper about moving you to another assignment."

"Please don't, Bart. Rachel and I can get along." They both turned to stare at me. "We just had a difference of opinion. Rachel is a good counselor and the girls really like her."

Bart looked at me long and hard. "I'm surprised you're sticking up for her, Mike. All right, I won't say anything for now. You two work this out."

"We will," Rachel and I chorused.

Bart walked away shaking his head. Rachel turned to me with a puzzled expression on her face. "Why did you stick up for me?" she asked.

"Believe it or not, Rachel, I like you." I did, too. Maybe if she hadn't been so much older than me, well… "I think you're a good sailor and a great counselor. I know Christy Ann really likes you, too." Much to my surprise, Rachel responded by hugging me. I gingerly put my arms around her and lightly returned her hug.

"Thanks, Mike," Rachel said. "And don't worry. Christy Ann will be on your boat. I wouldn't trust her with anyone else."

Now technically, it wouldn't be my boat. There would be four of us plus a counselor. The counselor would be the skipper.

"How would you feel about being on my boat?" Rachel asked.

"I think I'd like that," I told her, but I had a funny feeling about it.

"Good then," she smiled. "You and Christy Ann will be on my boat. Now, why don't you get back to the campfire before she decides you've abandoned her?"

Taking her advice, I returned to the campfire and found Christy Ann saving a spot for me.

"What in the world were you guys talking about for so long?" Christy Ann asked.

"We were discussing boat assignments for tomorrow," I told her as I settled back against the log.

"Really, it looked more like an argument than a discussion," Christy Ann observed. She moved so our shoulders touched.

"It was just a trick of the firelight." Changing the subject I told her, "Rachel wants us on her boat tomorrow."

"I'd like that," Christy Ann said. We watched the fire for a while, and then Christy Ann turned to me. "Do you think she's pretty?"

"Is who pretty?"

She elbowed me lightly. "You know who, Rachel. I saw her hug you. Do you think she's pretty?"

"I guess so," I replied. "I'm not really into older women. She's at least three years older than me."

Christy Ann smiled at me shyly. "How do you feel about girls your own age?"

I should have realized she was referring to herself, but my thoughts went immediately to Rhiannon. "I haven't had much luck in that age group either," I confessed with a sigh.

"Maybe your luck is about to change," Christy Ann said as she put her arm through mine and rested her head on my shoulder.

Finally catching her meaning, I turned to look at her. Her eyes were closed, but she had the cutest little smile on her face. I smiled down at her, and we stayed like that until the campfire was over.

We spent the next day teaching the novices how to sail the Flying Scotts. Scotts are nineteen-foot, open-cockpit sailboats that are a lot of fun to sail and easy to learn on. Christy Ann and I did wind up on Rachel's boat, and everything went fine. Rachel and I rigged the boat the first time, explaining as we did so exactly what we were doing and why.

Once the boat was ready, Rachel took control of the tiller and main sheet while I manned the jib sheets. We took the crew out on a three-point course to demonstrate how to tack and jibe the Scott around the buoys. Then the new sailors took turns at the helm and trimming the sails. We kept at it all day until each member of our crew, including Christy Ann, could handle the tiller, main sheet, or jib sheet confidently.

As dusk settled over the camp that evening, a thunderstorm rolled in from the southwest with a cold front behind it. Since campfires in the rain aren't much fun, the evening festivities were moved into the Camp Life Center. Someone found a record player and a few records, so we held an impromptu dance. I danced with most of the girls in my sailing group but found myself dancing with Christy Ann for all the slow songs.

Before the festivities wound down, Christy Ann told me she was feeling tired and asked me to walk her to her cabin. The rain had stopped by then, and there was a bit of a chill in the air. Christy Ann shivered a bit, so I put my arm around her shoulders. She moved closer to me and slipped her arm around my waist. When we got to her cabin, she turned to me and put both arms around me.

"Thanks, Mikey," she said as she hugged me and kissed my cheek. "I'll see you in the morning."

"I'll see you then," I said with a pleased grin on my face. "Sleep tight."

"I will." Christy Ann hesitated just a second before breaking into a big smile and hurrying into her cabin.

I stood there a minute or two looking at the closed door before turning and walking out onto the dock. There were some things I needed to think about. At thirteen there were some things about feelings I didn't understand.

Christy Ann had kissed me, on the cheek, but it was still a kiss, and I liked it. Did that make me disloyal to Rhiannon? I searched my heart. Did I still love Rhiannon? Yes. Did I love Christy Ann? I liked her, sure, but I was just as sure I wasn't in love with her. And it wasn't like I had kissed her, so, okay then. Feeling like I'd resolved the issue, I headed off to my cabin to get some sleep.

Four

The next morning dawned clear and cool. Cool for summer in North Carolina anyway, only 68 degrees. It wouldn't last, but while it did we intended to enjoy it. A brisk breeze from the northwest would make for some fun sailing. We spent the day on the water improving our skills with the Scotts. Our crews needed to be proficient as we would soon be making our first overnight excursion.

By the end of the day we were pronounced ready for that first overnight trip. After a dinner of fried chicken, mashed potatoes, and corn on the cob, we inspected and packed all the equipment we'd need for the excursion. Most of us skipped the campfire since we had an early departure time scheduled. Though the night air was warm, compared to the night before, I still put my arm around Christy Ann as I walked her to her cabin.

From the river came the sound of a power boat making its way slowly towards Pamlico Sound. We stopped and searched until we spotted its lights on the water. Christy Ann sighed contentedly and rested her head against my shoulder. "I'm really looking forward to our trip, Mikey."

"So am I," I told her, my eyes following the red and white lights of the all-but-invisible boat making its way down river. "Sailing is even more fun when you are going somewhere and not just sailing around and around."

Christy Ann turned her face up to me expectantly. "I'll see you in the morning."

"I'll see you then," I replied and bent over and kissed her oh so softly on the lips.

It wasn't very long or filled with passion, but it was a first kiss for both of us. Christy Ann beamed and gave me a cute little wave as she went into her cabin. I smiled and waved back, not leaving to go to my own cabin until the door closed behind her.

I suppose I should have felt more after my first kiss. All I could think was my first kiss should have been with Rhiannon. Still, I did like Christy Ann, and it was a nice kiss. It didn't mean I was in love with her.

The next morning at breakfast, Rachel asked to speak to me alone. She looked worried. I looked for Christy Ann among the girls walking toward the dining hall and didn't see her.

"Mike, Christy Ann won't be going with us on the overnight trip," Rachel said. She sounded worried.

"Why not?" I asked guardedly.

"She's in the infirmary. She began running a fever early this morning."

Fear crept into my gut. "What's the matter with her? She seemed fine when I walked her to the cabin last night."

"It came on suddenly," Rachel said, shaking her head slowly. "If it doesn't go down they'll probably take her to the hospital in New Bern."

"Can I go see her?" I was going to no matter what Rachel said.

"Only for a few minutes. We'll be leaving soon."

"All right, I'll meet you at the dock." I took my half-eaten breakfast to the scullery and hurried to the infirmary. The nurse on duty, Mrs. Jolyn, told me Christy Ann was sleeping.

"May I look in on her?" I asked, or more rightly, pleaded.

Mrs. Jolyn thought about it for a minute. "I guess it would be all right. Just be careful not to disturb her."

I moved to Christy Ann's bedside very quietly, only to discover she was awake.

"Hi," I said, forcing myself to smile. "What's the big idea of skipping out on our trip?"

"I'm sorry, Mikey," Christy Ann said, and then she started to cry. "I really wanted to go, too."

"Hey, it's all right." I took her hand and tried to comfort her. "We'll be going on lots more trips."

"I hope so Mikey." Squeezing my hand she added, "If I have to leave, Mikey, I'm glad of one thing."

"What's that?" I asked her, trying not to cry myself.

Christy Ann took a deep breath and smiled through her tears. "I'm glad you were my first kiss."

I could feel my tears starting. Swallowing hard I told her, "Me too, you were my first, too. If you hurry and get better we can have a second and maybe a third."

"I'd like that, Mikey," Christy Ann said softly.

Mrs. Jolyn came in and told me I should go. She needed to check Christy Ann's vitals.

Christy Ann looked up at me and put on a brave face. "You need to get going, Mikey, or you'll miss your boat. I'll see you when you get back."

Swallowing hard past the lump in my throat, I told her, "I hate to be going without you, Christy Ann."

"I love hearing you say that. Before you go maybe we could have our second kiss."

I smiled, bent down, and kissed her. It was a little more of a kiss than we'd had the night before. Mrs. Jolyn coughed lightly to remind us she was in the room, and I stood up straight. "You hurry and get better so you can make the next trip."

"I'll try, Mikey," Christy Ann promised.

"Okay then," I said. "I guess I've got to go."

"All right, Mikey. I'll see you when you get back." I kissed her quickly on the hand before turning to leave. As I started walking away Christy Ann said one more thing. "I love you, Mikey."

I stopped and turned back to her. I know she wanted me to say I loved her too. Looking into her eyes I knew that's what she expected me to say. I felt like I should, but how could I? It wouldn't be true. I liked Christy Ann a lot, but I didn't love her. If I loved anyone, it was Rhiannon. I didn't know what to do. Walking back to her bedside I took her hand. "You just get better so we can go sailing. I'll see you when I get back."

I turned away quickly but couldn't avoid seeing the disappointment in her eyes. She didn't say anything more as I walked out of the infirmary. Stopping by my cabin to pick up my dry bag, I finally made my way to the dock.

Rachel ran up to me as I started toward the boats. "How is she?"

"I don't know," I said, looking back toward the infirmary. "I hope she'll be all right."

Rachel touched me lightly on the arm. "So do I."

I don't know why I went ahead on that trip. It was just one more overnighter. I hardly remember it. When we got back I expected to see Christy Ann waiting for us on the dock. She wasn't there. Leaving the rest of the crew to take care of the boat, I headed to her cabin to see if she was there. Mr. Cooper met me at the head of the dock. He looked somber. "Michael," Mr. Cooper said sadly, "if you're looking for Christy Ann, I'm afraid she's gone."

I didn't get his meaning right away. "She left camp. Is she coming back?"

"No Michael, I mean she's gone, she passed away."

"She's dead," I said stunned. My whole body went numb. "How?"

"She was very sick, Michael. Coming to camp here was one of her last wishes," Mr. Cooper explained. "She didn't want anyone to know. She wanted to be treated like every other camper. Only Rachel, me, and Mrs. Jolyn knew."

Tears welled in my eyes. My legs went weak. I collapsed to the ground sobbing. I didn't want to believe it. Rachel walked up, saw me, and realized what must have happened. She sat down beside me and put her arm around me. Mr. Cooper left me there with her and went to tell the others what had happened. There were a lot of tears. It was the saddest day I ever knew at camp.

That night we had a special campfire in memory of Christy Ann. We each got up to tell something we would remember about her. We hadn't really known her long, but everyone remembered something they could share. I went last.

"Christy Ann quickly became my good friend. In the short time I knew her we shared many things. I probably shouldn't tell this, but we shared our first kiss right there in front of her cabin."

It was a moment before I could continue. "She was the first girl to ever tell me she loved me. She told me the morning when I went to see her before we left."

At this point I lost it; the tears just came. "But I didn't tell her I loved her. God help me, but I couldn't lie to her about that. What would it have hurt to say it? I'm sorry, Christy Ann. I'm so sorry."

I sat down and cried like a little boy. Rachel and Bart sat with me and tried to console me, but I had to get it out of my system, I guess.

It was several days before things returned to a semblance of normal. I found relief on the water, sailing. I prayed a lot when I was out there on the water and eventually worked through my grief.

Young hearts and minds rebound faster than most. By the end of camp I was almost back to my old self. Two weeks of sailing helped a lot with that. Sailing always soothed me.

Eventually it was time to go home. My memories of that summer at Camp would certainly be unlike any others. Though we had only a few days together, Christy Ann touched my life and heart in ways that would stay with me forever.

Five

August 1974

When I got home from Camp Riversail, the first person I wanted to see was Rhiannon. Memories of how sad she'd seemed when I left for Camp fueled a silly romantic idea in my thirteen-year-old head. The whole ride home I imagined Rhiannon realizing how much she'd missed me, admitting she did love me as much as I loved her, and the two of us finally becoming a real couple. Despite not getting home until late evening, I headed to the pier as soon as I could, anticipating a heartwarming reunion.

"Oh, hi, Mike, you back from camp already?" Rhiannon greeted me when she saw me come through the door. She was working behind the counter selling pier passes to the fisherman. That summer her dad decided thirteen was old enough to start working at, instead of just hanging out around, the pier.

Disappointed by her lackluster welcome, I managed to stammer out a reply. "Uh, yeah, um, I just got home. I came up here soon as my Mom let me."

"How was it?" She didn't sound particularly interested.

"Uh, it was different," I told her, not really wanting to get into the whole story right there at the register. "I missed you, though."

"You did?" she asked with a funny little grin.

"Yeah, I did. Did you miss me?"

"I guess so," she replied with a shrug. "My Dad's kept me pretty busy here."

"Well I don't want to keep you from your work," I said a bit sourly, turning to walk out.

"Michael, wait," Rhiannon called after me. I stopped and turned towards her. "I'm glad you're home, Mike. It's been kind of lonely around here without my best friend." There was that little grin again. "Can ya stick around?"

Not wanting to let on how glad I was she'd asked, I shrugged and struggled to keep the smile off my face. "I can stay for a little while."

Rhiannon gestured at the cash register. "Then come help me sell passes."

I slipped behind the counter and helped her until Uncle Lind came in from walking the pier. A warm smile crossed his lips when he saw us together behind the counter. He took her place at the register and told us to take the rest of the night off.

Rhiannon and I walked out onto the pier and found an empty bench. She wanted to know all about camp, and I told her about what happened to Christy Ann. I left out the part about what good friends Christy Ann and I had become in those few days. I didn't tell Rhiannon about the kiss and what Christy Ann said to me. Rhiannon told me what it had been like working at the pier instead of just hanging out.

"It's sad what happened to that girl, Michael."

"Yes, it was. It made for a very subdued camp experience."

We sat quietly together for several minutes until Rhiannon decided she needed to break me out of my funk. Eyes twinkling with mischief she teased, "Did you really miss me, Mike, with all those pretty girls around camp?"

"I hardly noticed them at all, Rhiannon. None of them were as pretty as you," but as I said it I thought of Christy Ann and felt a little stab of guilt.

Rhiannon rolled her eyes, "Michael, you are a nut."

"Rhiannon," I started to tell her I loved her. Instead I said, "Do you want to go sailing tomorrow?"

"I've got to work in the afternoon, but we can go in the morning."

"Great, come to the house and we'll take out the Sunfish for a quick cruise," I said.

"Okay, Mike, I'll be there."

"Great, then it's a date."

"We're just going sailing, Michael. Don't get any ideas."

"I'm full of ideas, Rhiannon," I said, setting myself up for her next line.

"You're full of it all right, Michael," Rhiannon laughed.

"Fery vunny, Rhiannon, I love you too," I said laughing along with her.

"I know you do, Michael," Rhiannon said as she headed into the pier house. I sat there not knowing what to think of that. Finally I decided it was time to head home. When I got to the pier house Rhiannon had already said good night to her dad and gone to their house. I walked on home.

That's pretty much how it went right through the end of ninth grade. Rhiannon and I hung out and did lots of things together, but we never dated. I made it pretty plain how I felt about her and was rather persistent. She did not relent with her rules. Then again, she never told me to take a hike either. As ninth grade ended I tried one last time, that rainy night by the pinball machine.

"Rhiannon, you know the Ninth Grade Social is coming up." The Ninth Grade Social was sort of our prom. We spent freshman year at a ninth-grade-only center. The Social was our final school-related social event before we all went on to high school in the fall.

"Yes, Michael, I know and no, Michael, I won't go with you," Rhiannon preempted me.

"What makes you think I was going to ask you?" I said, even though I knew she knew I was.

"Just a wild guess," she replied with a dismissive chuckle.

"Why not? Rhiannon, I'm crazy about you. You know that. I love you. Why won't you?"

She took a deep breath and let it out slowly. "Michael, we've been over this. You know you are my best friend. I want it to stay that way. What if we start dating and it doesn't work out? We couldn't be friends anymore afterwards. Michael, this isn't one of those 'let's just be friends' speeches. I do love you and I love being your best friend. I'm just not ready for a boyfriend. It's not just you. Haven't you been paying attention? I haven't dated anyone. I'm not ready for that, yet."

"What if I said that if you won't go out with me then we can't be friends anymore?" I challenged and immediately regretted it when I saw the fear and hurt in her eyes.

In a quiet voice she said, "I don't think you would do that, not if you really love me."

Wishing I could take it back, I reached out and took her hand. "You're right, Rhiannon, I could never tell you that. I could never do that."

She didn't pull her hand away. "You will still go to the dance, right?"

Despite the warm feeling of her hand in mine, I still wasn't sure about going to the dance. "I don't know…"

"Please, go," Rhiannon pleaded. "I'll be there, with no date, and will need someone to dance with."

Unable to say no, I told her, "I'll be there."

"Save the last dance for me," she said.

I did.

Six

August 1976

"Owen, is Michael out of bed yet?" my mom asked my dad while standing at the stove tending a skillet full of eggs. My mother, Eunice Lanier, was a tall, angular woman who always seemed to have a serious expression on her face. The roots of her dark brown hair were just beginning to show gray. I inherited my blue eyes from her.

Dad replied from behind his newspaper. "I heard him working out on his deck, dear. I'm sure he'll be down directly." Owen Lanier, my dad, was one inch taller than my mother, but the way she wore her hair most of the time she looked taller. Dad's hair was jet black, with flecks of gray starting to show here and there.

"I hope so. I would not want him to be late for his first day of high school." School attendance was important to my mother. Twelve years of perfect attendance records were safely stored in her cedar chest, along with her other mementos. She'd probably had perfect attendance to all her classes at Wellesley, too.

As I bounded down the stairs into the kitchen I assured her, "I won't be late. See, here I am ready to go."

Gesturing toward the skillet with her spatula, she informed me, "You are not leaving before you have a good breakfast; it is the most important meal of the day. I have scrambled you some eggs, fried some bacon, and there is an English muffin for you in the toaster."

My mother never used contractions. I never learned why. Perhaps it was something she picked up at Wellesley. Maybe she thought it made her sound more refined than someone who grew up over a bakery in a small southwestern New Hampshire town might otherwise be expected to sound.

"Thanks, mom," I said, giving her a kiss on the cheek and taking a seat at the table.

My father lowered his paper and leveled his pale green eyes on me. "Think you're ready for high school, Michael?"

"I think so, Dad."

"Do you have all your notebooks and such you are supposed to bring today?" Mom asked.

I pointed with my fork toward the stack of binders on the table by the door. "Yes, ma'am, I sure do."

My mother looked at me with a skeptical expression, as if deciding whether to take my word for it, before smiling and giving me a pat on the shoulder.

"Then eat your breakfast. You need to get moving or you will miss your bus."

"You sure you don't want me to drive you to school, Michael?" Dad offered. My mother frowned at him in disapproval.

"I'm sure, Dad. I've been riding the bus all these years. It won't hurt me any the next couple of months."

Though there were a number of private schools I could have attended, my parents wouldn't allow it. They strongly believed an important part of getting a complete education included getting to know, and learning how to deal with, people from a wide variety of backgrounds.

My father explained it this way. "People are people. What makes us different is what we learn while we grow up. What you learn in class is important, but life's most important lessons aren't learned from books; they're learned from your experiences, the people around you, at home, in the neighborhood, wherever you find yourself. Those experiences are what help make you who you are."

"Follow the Golden Rule," was my mom's simple, straightforward advice. I learned over time there were two golden rules: the one my mother made reference to and the one that says he who has the gold makes the rules. Fortunately, through a strange quirk of fate, I had more than my fair share of gold.

During World War One my mother's father fought in France with the Allied Expeditionary Force. During a rather fierce engagement, he risked his life to save the life of a home-town friend named Michael Justin. Corporal Justin survived his wounds, thanks to my grandfather, and they stayed in touch and remained friends after the war.

Mr. Justin inherited a little money from his father. With that and what he had saved during the war, he went into the real estate business. He did exceedingly well. Using some of his investments, he helped finance the growing utilities companies forming around the region. Those investments did even better. He foresaw the storm clouds forming over Wall Street before the Great Depression and got out of the market early, sheltering his assets from that catastrophe.

During World War Two he invested in war production and saw his fortune grow enormously. After the war, Mr. Justin made savvy investments as the returning war veterans went to school on the GI Bill and created a growing middle class of new consumers.

Mr. Justin had it all, except a wife and family. The nature of his war injury prevented him from ever fathering children, so he never got married and instead devoted all his time and energy to his business enterprises.

All during this time he and my grandfather remained friends. Grandpa returned from the war, bought a small bakery, and built up a good business providing fresh goods to customers all over town. He made a good living and provided well for my grandmother and their three daughters. Mr. Justin was like a second father to my mom and her two older sisters. He wanted to spoil them rotten, but my grandfather was pretty strict about it.

My mother's oldest sister, my Aunt Deloris, was widowed at a young age and never had any children. She never remarried. The middle sister, my Aunt Debra, went to teachers' college, became a teacher, and also never married. My mom met a sailor whom she did marry and who, in good time became my dad.

To honor both my grandfather and his old friend, they were going to name me Justin Michael, but at grandpa's insistence they changed it to Michael Justin. So, though Michael Justin had no heirs of his own, he did have me to carry his name. At my baptism mom and dad named him my Godfather.

Unknown to any of them, Mr. Justin set up a trust fund for me and made me his sole heir. He knew some very high-powered lawyers who drew it all up so it would be virtually unbreakable and incontestable. They were very good at what they did. Then he set up a fund which would pay them to watch over it all in perpetuity. Not only that, he put another firm in control of the investments and disbursements and set up a fund which would pay them, too. He included a requirement that both the law firm and the investment firm had to have outside independent reviews every so often to make sure they followed the terms.

To counter having inherited all that, once they learned of it, my parents made darn sure I never let it go to my head. They kept me on a pretty tight fiscal leash and did not hesitate to remind me I had not earned it. That doesn't mean I had a deprived childhood. We lived in a nice house on the sound in Wrightsville Beach. I went to summer camps where I learned to boat, sail, scuba dive, kayak, climb up mountains, rappel back down them, and just about any other outdoor pursuit a growing boy could hope for. With my family I spent vacations seeing America and the world. Thanks to my dad and his brothers, I learned how to hunt, fish, and respect the outdoors. Most important of all, thanks to my parents and my Grandpa Justin, I learned how to respect the great gift I had been given. That last Wednesday of August 1976, I hoped all this had prepared me for what lay ahead, High School.

Seven

I woke up at six that morning, my usual time. Sticking with my morning routine, I walked out onto the deck extending from my loft and overlooking the sound. There I stretched and did my morning exercises. The morning air was warm and muggy, foretelling a hot, humid day.

I took a cool shower before pulling on a pair of blue jeans and a light gray Camp Riversail t-shirt. Slipping my sockless feet into a well worn pair of Top Sider boat shoes, I checked myself in the mirror and winced a bit. My sun-bleached, light brown hair was cut shorter than I liked, but there was nothing I could do about that. Short hair was required for Junior ROTC. Deciding that, other than the hair, I looked presentable, I headed downstairs.

After wolfing down the breakfast my mother prepared, I walked to the end of our short road where the bus stopped to pick up Rhiannon and me. We were at the end of the route. Rhiannon, looking very pretty in a white peasant blouse with a lace collar and tiny, colorful flowers embroidered across the chest, greeted me with a smile as I walked up.

"Good morning, Mike, ready for high school?"

Rhiannon had been a gangly kid but had grown into a beautiful young lady. She often wore her auburn hair, which reached past her shoulders, in a ponytail as she did that morning. While this allowed her to show off her lovely face and dazzling green eyes, I always thought her more attractive when she let it hang free. I was scandalized when she told me she was going to cut it off for cheerleading because she thought it got in the way. I was relieved when she didn't.

Rhiannon and I had been friends since forever, but she would never consent to be my girlfriend. She would laugh and say she was a girl and my friend but she couldn't be my girlfriend. Rhiannon had rules about not being your best friend's girlfriend. I had more or less given up trying around the end of Ninth Grade.

Grinning now as I approached the bus stop, I replied, "Ever ready, that's me, just like the batteries. How 'bout you?"

"Ready as I can be, mon ami," Rhiannon laughed. We chatted for a while about what freshman year was going to be like.

"I can't believe we don't have any classes together," I moaned dramatically.

Rhiannon rolled her eyes. "Well, you had to go and take Spanish instead of French this year," she reminded me. "What were you thinking?"

I rubbed my chin as though giving the matter a great deal of consideration. "I was thinking it would be fun to be able to speak Spanish and French."

Rhiannon rolled her eyes and shook her head. "Hans said you should have taken German."

"I will senior year. It's all in the plan."

After picking us up, the bus drove to the end of South Lumina Avenue and around the cul-de-sac by the Coast Guard Station before heading back over the bridges to Wilmington. Wrightsville Beach did not have a big enough population to warrant its own high school. In fact, New Hanover County had just that summer finished building only its third high school, Laney High School, my high school.

So there we were on that Wednesday morning, Rhiannon and me, on the school bus headed for our first day of high school on Laney's first ever student day. It wasn't actually my first day at Laney as I had been going out every day for a week for soccer practice. In the coach's mind I was probably eleventh string since I'd been out of town until a week before and missed the first two weeks of practice. With luck, he would at least keep me on the roster as second assistant backup junior varsity manager. Really, though, I had nothing to worry about. They needed at least eleven players, and only a dozen others besides my friend Hans and me showed up to play.

Anyway, there we were on the bus. It was not a long ride to the school as such things go. Our ride downtown to the Virgo Ninth Grade Center had been longer. Our long ride, time wise, would be in the afternoon when we were the last dropped off and had to sit through all the other stops. Between my soccer practice and Rhiannon's cheerleading practice, we didn't ride the bus home too many afternoons.

To get to the high school the bus had to cross two bridges, one over the sound and one over the waterway. In between the two bridges was Harbor Island. Then it was up Eastwood Road to Market Street and a sharp turn onto the ramp to the overpass to College Road. Laney High was on College Road at the north end of the county. Soon, the big yellow bus pulled into the bus lot behind the school and off we went.

Thanks to the new student orientation session the week before, I already knew where my homeroom was and how to get there. My homeroom teacher was Miss Tomlinson; or should I say Senorita Tomlinson, since she was also my Spanish Teacher. All my other classes were of the ordinary tenth grade variety: Algebra 2, Chemistry, Composition, Social Studies. Of course there was Spanish 1, and just to be different, Naval Junior Reserve Officers' Training Corp, better known as JROTC. Having earned my Eagle Scout rank by the time I was fifteen, JROTC seemed like the next logical uniformed step. That's six classes, and we had seven periods. The extra period was for the most important class, lunch.

Homeroom started at eight. At three-twenty the final bell rang. Soccer practice was from three-thirty to five. Ninety minutes was plenty the way Coach Donaldson ran us. After practice either my mom or dad would pick me up. No special buses to take athletes home from practic.

Once games started we would play on Tuesday and Thursday, practice on Monday and Wednesday, and have Fridays off with the expectation we would be at the Varsity Football games. Due to the small number of players, there was no junior varsity soccer team. It was just us.

The first day the bus managed to get us to school a few minutes early, so we waited in the area between the gym and the main building before the doors opened. The Laney campus then consisted of four buildings. The main building was two stories laid out in a square around a courtyard. Classrooms lined both sides of all eight halls but one. The eighth hall is where the administrative offices were, on the first floor opposite the gym.

The second building was the gym. Besides the gymnasium it housed the locker rooms, a weight room, health classroom, and the coach's offices. There were also storage rooms for the sports equipment, and on the back of the gym were the maintenance and custodial rooms. The third building, located 180 degrees across the main building from the gym, was the cafeteria. This building also included the chorus and band rooms and the school store.

The fourth building was the vocational education building. The room that would be my homeroom my junior year, the electrical studies room, was in this building. So was the JROTC Classroom, with its associated armory, storage room, and offices. There was also a wood shop, an auto shop, and an art room.

Athletic fields included a football stadium that doubled for a soccer field, baseball and softball fields, and tennis courts. Promised at some unspecified date in the future were a running track and a dedicated soccer field. I never saw either while I was there.

My sophomore homeroom, Senorita Tomlinson's classroom, was located on the second floor hall opposite the cafeteria. Once they opened the building Rhiannon and I headed that way. Her homeroom teacher, Mrs. Nadeau the French teacher, had the room next to Senorita Tomlinson. Hans' homeroom was across the hall with Frau Gerhard, the German teacher. Somehow he got in early and was waiting for us outside Frau Gerhard's door.

"Man, I cannot believe you're taking German," I chided him. "You already speak German."

"It should be an easy A for me then, yes? Why didn't you take German?"

Smiling a confident grin I replied, "It's part of the long-range plan. I'll take it senior year after I get Spanish down."

"First French and now Spanish, you're hoping for a job at the United Nations I think."

Leaving Hans chuckling at his own joke, I crossed the hall to my homeroom. Before she continued down the hall to Mrs. Nadeau's room, Rhiannon surprised me with a quick hug.

"Good luck, Mike, I'll see you at lunch."

Clearly amused by my startled expression, she spun about and hurried to class. I muttered "good luck to you, too" at her retreating back.

Miss Tomlinson greeted each one of us with an enthusiastic "Buenos Dias" as we walked in her door. I responded with a very southern "Bwainos Diaz" and hurried to find my seat. If I hadn't already met her at orientation, it might have been hard to tell Miss Tomlinson from her students. She was very young and very pretty.

I found a seat next to another pretty young lady. She had shoulder-length hair the color of winter wheat, and when I turned to say hello I noticed her eyes were the most incredible shade of amber. Her name, I soon learned, was Jill Jonas.

Jill was new to the area. Her family moved to Porter's Neck from Asheville over the summer because of her dad's new job at the General Electric plant. Jill and I hit it off right away, and I remember thinking maybe there was hope for high school yet.

Spanish class didn't really get started that first day because of all the administrative nonsense we had to clear up and go over first. I didn't care, nor did any of the other boys in class. We were quite content to sit and listen to Senorita Tomlinson and wouldn't have cared if she'd been reciting the phone book. I don't think the girls were quite as captivated.

"This is what I hate about the first day of school," Jill commented in a bored tone.

"All this paperwork and stuff?" I asked holding up my stack of forms.

"Yeah, all this stuff," Jill said in a way to clearly indicate she was calling it stuff to be polite. Then she turned to me with a sly smile. "I notice you were able to give it your full attention."

"I wanted to be sure I didn't miss anything important."

Jill didn't look convinced, and I felt color rise in my cheeks. "Oh, I'm sure you didn't," she laughed.

Class ended and I waited for her to walk out. When she stood up I was surprised to find she was quite tall, almost as tall as me.

She chuckled and shook her head when I bowed and swept my arm to indicate she should precede me from the classroom. Glancing back over her shoulder, she caught me watching, winked, and hurried out the door.

My second class was Algebra 2. I was able to take Geometry in ninth grade because I'd qualified for Algebra 1 in eighth grade. Hans was also in the Algebra 2 class.

"So, Mike, how goes it so far?" he asked as I took the seat next to his.

"So far, so good," I said, smiling as I thought of Jill. "I met a new girl in Spanish."

This peaked Hans' interest. "Did you, and her name would be?"

"Jill, Jill Jonas."

Hans looked thoughtful for a moment. "I do not think I know her."

I nodded. "She moved here from Asheville over the summer."

"So, did you ask her out?"

I didn't get a chance to answer as Mr. Burton, our Algebra 2 teacher, gave us one of those looks that says it's time to stop talking and listen. Satisfied he had our attention, he covered the syllabus for the class and launched into the first lesson.

"I know you didn't expect we would jump right into the material, but we have a lot to cover and no time to waste." He wasn't kidding.

On the way from Algebra 2 to third period class, I saw Mrs. Nadeau, the French teacher, for the first time. What caught my attention was her long, black hair. I thought she was a student until she turned around. She didn't look old, but she definitely didn't look like a high school girl.

Mrs. Nadeau was pretty hot, especially for a teacher. Unlike Miss Tomlinson, Mrs. Nadeau did not blend in with her students.

Much like Miss Tomlinson she most definitely had no trouble keeping the attention of the boys in her class. Of medium height and shapely build, it was Mrs. Nadeau's face, more than her other perfectly proportioned features that caught my attention. She had almond-shaped eyes, that were brown and flecked with gold, and long, perfect lashes. Her smile, while friendly, hinted that she found the attention she got from the boys amusing but not to be taken seriously. A deep tan spoke of hours spent on the beach in the summer sun. Barely noticeable wrinkles at the corners of her eyes said she was, perhaps, older than she appeared. Jennifer Nadeau was the most beautiful woman I had ever seen.

For a moment I wished I'd taken French 3 with Rhiannon instead of Spanish 1. I stuttered out a "Bon Jour, Madame" as I went by. Mrs. Nadeau replied, "Bon Jour, Monsieur," with a chuckle in her voice, somehow sounding very French, and very southern, at the same time.

Third period was Chemistry with Miss Royalle. Fourth period was ROTC. I had to hustle to make it to this class as it was in the back of the furthest building. I enjoyed ROTC as it was a real change from the other classes I was taking. Chief Spencer was a retired submariner. I thought that was pretty cool. Walking into the room, I realized there wasn't a single person in the class I knew well. A couple people I recognized from Virgo.

One guy who didn't look familiar was sitting alone on the far side of the room. I walked over and introduced myself. "Hey, man, I'm Mike."

He looked up as if startled and regarded me for a second. Finally he put out his hand and said, "Hi Mike, I'm Wesley. My friends call me Wes."

Shaking his hand I replied, "Nice to meet you, Wes. Did you go to Virgo?" I asked, though I was pretty sure he hadn't.

Wes confirmed this when he said, "No, I went to school in Jacksonville. My dad just retired from the Marines."

"That's cool, is he from around here?"

"Nah, he got offered a job at Corning when he retired from the Corps, so we moved here last July."

Chief Spencer walked in just then and stood in the door glaring at us. I quickly took the seat behind Wes.

"As you people will learn, it is traditional in the Navy to come to attention when the person in charge walks into a room," Chief growled before turning around and walking away. We all looked at each other. Wes watched the door. Shortly Chief returned.

"Class, attention," Wes called out and then jumped to his feet. Since I figured he knew what he was doing, his father being a Marine and all, I stood too. The rest of the class wisely followed his lead as well.

Chief glared at each of us before informing us in a voice dripping with disappointment, "That was about as sloppy a coming to attention as I have ever seen, but we'll work on it. At ease, take your seats."

Such was my introduction to NJROTC. On top of the homeroom forms we had to take home, Chief gave us more. These had to do with uniforms, military matters, and a code of conduct for cadets. He told us some of what the class would be like. This spiel was much like the one he'd given at Virgo the spring before, the one I heard that made me decide to take the class.

Fifth period was my favorite, lunch. Since fifth period was the sophomore lunch all my friends ate then too. We laid claim to a table near the windows, one of the big round ones that would hold our whole group: Hans and his off-again-on-again girlfriend April, Beth Bosworth, who was running late, Wesley from my ROTC class, and of course, Rhiannon. Jill came in and I invited her to join us at our table. She had Chorus fourth period, so her class was just around the corner from the cafeteria.

Jill eyed us cautiously. "Are you sure there's room?" she asked, noting one empty chair across the table from me.

Hans, acting like a gentleman, responded, "Sure there is." He rose and got her a chair from another table. Wedging it between Rhiannon and me he said, "Right here next to Michael."

"Well, okay," Jill said with a smile, "Hi, everyone."

Rhiannon moved her chair over to make room for Jill after casting an evil glance at Hans. Hans was more concerned with the evil look coming his way from his girlfriend. He shrugged an apology in April's direction and sat back down. I introduced Jill to our little group, and they each introduced themselves.

Beth joined us a few minutes later, filling out our table. "Hi, everyone, sorry I'm late. Mr. Pringle held us over in band. Figures, I'm just down the hall from the cafeteria, and I'm the last one to get here."

Beth was an accomplished musician even at that age. She could play the flute, the clarinet, the saxophone, the piano, and the guitar. She could probably play more instruments, but those are the ones I remember. Beth was a cute, petite blond with lots of spirit and energy.

"Well, at least you made it," I said. "Beth, this is Jill Jonas."

Beth eyed Jill for a moment, taking in her location between Rhiannon and me. Then she looked at me and raised a questioning eyebrow. Finally she turned back to Jill. "Hi Jill, how do you like it here so far?"

Beth's hesitation made Jill a bit uncomfortable. She looked at me out of the corner of her eye, but I wasn't really paying attention. To Beth she said, "So far it's been pretty good. Everyone's been really nice."

Beth took her seat. "Well I'm glad to hear that. Most people get to know these two here," she pointed to Hans and me, "and run for their lives."

"Well, just thank you very much, Miss Beth," Hans said indignantly.

Looking up from my toasted cheese sandwich, I echoed Hans. "Yeah, Beth, thanks bunches."

Jill laughed and took me by the arm. "I'm sure they're mostly harmless."

I saw Beth's eyes dart to Rhiannon and looked that way. Rhiannon was sitting stiffly in her seat looking at Jill's hand on my arm. No one else seemed to have noticed. Beth smiled at Jill. "Yeah, the boys are mostly harmless." Everyone laughed at this and we all got back to the important business of scarfing down our lunch before the bell rang.

Sixth period was Composition. Beth was in this class with me, so we walked there together after lunch. "So, Mike, have you asked Jill out yet?" Beth asked.

"No, I'm still waiting for you to dump that football player and go out with me," I teased.

"You know that's not going to happen. Greg and I have been together since seventh grade," Beth reminded me.

Sighing a melodramatic sigh I said, "I know, but you can't blame a guy for trying. Besides, he's at New Hanover High this year."

"Are you still trying to get Rhiannon to go out with you?" Beth asked, hoping to change the subject.

That chilled my mood. "Sadly, after all these years, I've given up."

"Michael, I know lots of girls who would love for you to ask them out. Why don't you?"

"I guess I'm really a coward at heart," I confessed, placing my hands over my heart.

"So, Mike, are you going to ask Jill out or not?" Beth asked again.

"What makes you think she'll go out with me?"

"Boy, are you dense. She did everything at lunch but put a lip lock on you. She'll go out with you. Take it from a girl who's had to tell you' no' when she wanted to say 'yes.' Jill will go out with you if you ask her."

"If you keep saying no when you want to say yes, why don't you dump Greg and go out with me?" I asked with a chuckle.

"Mike, it is not going to happen. I'm with Greg. Now, are you going to ask her out or are you going to let that ship sail?"

"Just so you know, I'm going to ask her if she wants to come to the football game and then go with us to Mikey's Friday night."

"You are, huh, Why didn't you just say so?"

"And miss all this delightful give and take we share? No way."

Beth turned into Miss Preston's room. "You, Michael, are a brat."

With a resigned sigh, I watched her go to her seat. "I hear that a lot."

Miss Preston could have been chosen by Central Casting as a spinster school teacher from the 1870s. She seemed at least 100 years old, though we never did learn just how old she was. As far as we knew she had never married. Teaching had been her whole life; specifically, teaching writing. She was very good at it. Her teaching style just resonated with most students, and they really worked hard for her approval.

Seventh period, the end of the day, was Social Studies. In tenth grade we studied US History prior to World War I, beginning with a section on Pre-Columbian American civilizations. It was taught by

Ms. Adkins. Make sure you use Ms, not Miss or Mrs. You better use Ms. I found this class fascinating. Hans and Jill were both in class with me. I managed to get a seat between them.

As we were leaving class, I took Jill aside. "Jill, are you coming to the football game Friday night?"

"I was planning to. Why?" Jill replied.

Having rehearsed in my head the ultra-cool way I was going to ask her, all that came out was, "I was thinking maybe we could meet at the game and sit together."

"Kind of like a date?" Jill asked, a smile lighting up her face.

"Well, yeah, like a date," I managed to say, "and after the game… do you know a place at the beach called Mikey's?"

"No, I don't think so," Jill said after a moment's thought. "Is it at Wrightsville Beach?"

"Yeah, it's kind of a night club for teens. We're all going there Friday night after the football game. Would you like to come with us?"

Jill scrunched her brow in thought. "I'll have to check with my folks. How would we get there?"

This was the awkward part. Since I wasn't 16 yet, one of my parents would have to take us from the game to Mikey's. My dad had already offered to give us a lift in his Suburban. With the third row of seats in he could take eight.

"My dad would drive us from the game to Mikey's. He's got a Suburban, and all our crowd fits. There'd be room for you."

The look on her face told me she was warming up to the idea. "But how would I get home?"

"Most of the parents pick up, but I'm sure my dad could drive us to your house and drop you off."

"I'd really like to, but I'll have to check with my parents. I'll let you know tomorrow." It was almost more of a question.

Jill's answer was close enough to a yes for me. Glancing over my shoulder, I told her, "Great, I need to catch up to Hans, soccer practice."

"Okay, see you tomorrow," Jill said. Then, much to my surprise, she kissed me on the cheek. She hurried off before I could react.

I had to hurry myself if I didn't want to be late for soccer practice. As I broke into a run I noticed Miss Tomlinson and Mrs. Nadeau watching me with amused smiles on their faces. I could only imagine what they were thinking.

Much to my surprise, during a water break I noticed Jill in the bleachers watching us practice. I guess she was waiting for her ride. It must have arrived right after that as she was gone the next time I looked. Coach didn't work us too hard as we had our first game of the season the next day, an away game against North Brunswick. We left practice in high spirits with high hopes.

I survived my first day of high school. Once home I got all the paperwork, and Mr. Burton's homework, out of the way so I could go to the pier. I hoped to see Rhiannon, but she wasn't working.

Walking out onto the pier, I ran into Hans and his mom. Mrs. Schultz came to the pier almost every night the weather allowed. Mr. Schultz worked second shift, so fishing gave her something to do and she really enjoyed it.

After asking Mrs. Schultz how the fishing was, Hans and I walked to the end of the pier. Hans punched me lightly on the shoulder. "So, did you ask Jill out?"

Giving Hans an annoyed look, I reminded him. "I asked her to the game. I told you at soccer practice."

"Yes, yes you did. And you told Beth you were going to ask Jill out. Did you mention anything to Rhiannon?" Hans' tone made it clear he suspected I had not.

"No, I didn't get to see her after lunch. Why would she care? It's not like she'll go out with me."

"That's true I suppose, but Rhiannon didn't look too happy with the way Jill replaced her at your side at the lunch table."

"You're crazy," I said. Then I remembered the way she stiffened up when Jill took my arm. "Besides, she should blame you. You're the one who put Jill's chair right there."

Hans chuckled at the memory. "Are you indicating that the seating arrangement wasn't to your liking?"

"No," I said with an exaggerated shake of my head. "I liked it just fine, and I think Jill liked it just fine, but if Rhiannon didn't like it I hope she knows to blame you and not me."

Eight

The second day of high school started much like the first, only it held the anticipation of two major events. One would affect the whole school. Our soccer game wasn't just the soccer team's first game; it would be the first athletic contest any Laney Buccaneer would ever compete in.

The other major event was of a much more personal nature. I would find out if Jill's parents were going to let her go with me to the football game and, more importantly, to Mikey's afterward. As I stood waiting at the end of my street, it seemed like the darn bus was never gonna get there. Rhiannon noticed my distracted look but guessed the wrong reason.

"Hey Mike, you ready for the big game today?"

Shaking my head to clear it, I answered absently, "Uh, yeah, I guess."

"'Uh, yeah,' what is that?" She didn't sound pleased by my response.

"What?"

"Never mind." She turned away with a disgusted look on her face. Then it hit me. I leaned over and whispered, "Ever ready, that's me, just like the batteries."

"Kind of late, but I'll forgive you," Rhiannon said with a smug look on her face. "Your brain is all befuddled with thoughts of your new love." That was definitely sarcastic.

Giving her my best innocent smile, I feigned ignorance. "What are you talking about? If my brain is befuddled by any love, it is my unrequited love for you, dear Rhiannon."

The bus arrived. We climbed aboard and took our usual seat. Once the bus got underway Rhiannon looked sideways at me. "Mike, you are certifiably insane, do you know that?"

"So I've often been told," I said dejectedly, looking down at my hands.

Rhiannon nudged me with her elbow, a little harder than might be considered polite. "You asked Jill out, didn't you?" There was a bit of an edge to her voice.

"Who've you been talking to?" I asked this, though I was pretty sure Beth had called her with the news. Then again, it could've been Hans. They'd been friends nearly as long as Rhiannon and me.

Rhiannon shook her head and grinned. "I asked you first. Now did you or didn't you?"

The look on her face made me kind of mad. "Did I or didn't I? Only my hairdresser knows for sure."

"You chickened out, didn't you?" Rhiannon stated with an oddly satisfied smile.

"As a matter of fact, and contrary to some people's opinions of my courage, I did not chicken out. I asked Jill to go with me to the game tomorrow night and," here I paused for dramatic effect, "to go with me to Mikey's afterward. So there."

"And what did she say?" If I was hoping for some kind of jealous reaction, Rhiannon wasn't giving me the satisfaction. Her voice betrayed no emotion at all.

"She answered with a resounding 'I'd really like to but I'll have to ask my parents.' Then she kissed me on the cheek." Despite myself, that memory made me smile.

Rhiannon considered that for a moment. "Well, it's better than a 'gee I don't know I'll have to ask my parents.'"

"It is, why?" They didn't seem different to me.

"Of course it is. Don't you know anything? 'I'd really like to but I'll have to ask my parents' means she really wants to but isn't sure her parents will let her. 'Gee I don't know I'll have to ask my parents' means she doesn't really want to but doesn't want to tell you to your face and is setting it up to blame her parents for not letting her go out with you. Besides, dummy, girls don't usually kiss someone they DON'T want to go out with."

Looking out the window behind Rhiannon, I noted we'd already crossed the draw bridge and were heading up Eastwood Road. "Is there a book or something you get all this out of, because if there is I'd really like to read it?"

Rhiannon shook her head and explained, slowly. "Michael, Michael, most girls won't just tell you 'no' like I will. They want to spare your feelings."

I sagged back against the seat with an exasperated sigh. "Whereas you have been perfectly happy to trample my feelings into the dirt all these years."

"Exactly," she replied with a forced laugh. I didn't think it was funny.

I took a mental inventory of my situation. The girl I liked most, Rhiannon, who was also my best friend, wouldn't go out with me even though to my knowledge she'd never had a boyfriend, and I'd known her since before we could walk. To make matters worse, she apparently thought it was fun trampling my feelings into the dirt.

Another girl I kind of liked, Beth, would go out with me, only she liked the guy she was already going out with just a little more than she did me, even though years ago she would have gone out with me if only I had asked her before he did. Or was Beth just saying that because, unlike Rhiannon, she did want to spare my feelings?

Now a new girl, Jill, entered the picture. A girl whom the first two girls seemed bound and determined I should go out with. At least I thought Rhiannon wanted me to think she thought I should go out with Jill. Jill, according to Beth and Rhiannon, really wanted to go out with me but couldn't until her parents signed off on the idea. In the midst of all this was the fact I hadn't had a steady girl-friend since…ever.

Rhiannon was eyeing me thoughtfully. "You're thinking, aren't you? I can smell the smoke."

Heaving a heavy sigh, I asked, "Rhiannon, why can't I find a girlfriend?"

Rhiannon shook her head sadly. "Because, dummy, you don't ask all the girls who want to go out with you. You keep asking those who can't."

"I'll grant that in Beth's case, but what about you?"

Rhiannon turned toward the window, and her shoulders slumped. "Trust me, Michael, it wouldn't work out. I love you like a brother, but you're not my type."

I was confused, but smart enough to know when not to pursue an issue, and this was definitely not the time to pursue that issue. Besides, we were pulling into the school lot and it was time to get off the bus.

"I'll see you later, Mike. There's something I've got to take care of." Rhiannon ran off before I could say anything. Instead I went looking for Jill. I found Hans.

"What's the matter with Rhiannon?" Hans asked as he watched her disappear around the corner of the gym.

"I'm not sure. She started out asking me if I asked Jill out and then lectured me about how I don't understand women. Finally she told me the reason she never went out with me is because I'm not her type."

Hans squinted one eye and looked at me carefully with the other. "She went through all that on the ride here?"

"Yep." Shifting my grip on my books, I turned and started walking towards the building.

"Most odd," Hans commented as he fell into step beside me. "So, did you ask Jill out? Oh, right, you already told me."

A short, sharp laughed slipped out. "Yes, yes I did. Now I'm looking for her to find out if she can go."

From behind me a voice sounded. "I can go, but you'll have to meet my dad when he drops me off for the game." I turned around to see Jill, and suddenly she was hugging me. "Isn't that great? I know he'll say it's okay once he meets you. I told him what a great guy you are."

Hans assumed a scandalized expression. "Jill, what will your father say when he actually meets Michael and learns the truth?"

Turning a disgusted look on him, I shot back, "Thanks a lot, best friend of mine."

"I thought I was your best friend," Beth said as she walked up.

I acted shocked. "Whatever made you think that?"

"She has a very high opinion of herself," Wesley put in, walking up beside her. They rode the same bus.

Beth looked from me to Wes and laughed. "You're both brats, you know? Jill, why do we give them the time of day?"

"We must be gluttons for punishment," Jill said. Then her expression softened. "I'm even dating one of them."

Raising her eyebrows, Beth asked, as if she didn't already know, "Really, which one?"

Jill put her arm possessively around me. "This one here."

Beth nodded in approval. "At least you got the pick of the litter."

This elicited a good natured chorus of bruised ego comments from the other guys, but I noticed something wistful in Beth's voice as she finished the jab. I looked at her inquiringly, but the bell rang just then. She turned and headed to the building. Jill and I walked to homeroom together.

"That seemed like a funny thing for Beth to say."

"She was just cracking wise." I was pretty sure that was all there was to it.

"I think she likes you more than she lets on," Jill observed.

"Beth and I have known each other since seventh grade. She's been Greg's girlfriend the whole time. Sometimes I think they were born engaged. She's a good friend."

As we reached our home room class, I saw Rhiannon going into Mrs. Nadeau's door. I started to walk down there to talk to her but stopped; it wasn't the time. Jill noticed.

"What about you and Rhiannon?"

"I've known Rhiannon practically my whole life. She's like a sister to me." There was nothing to be gained by telling Jill I'd been hopelessly in love with Rhiannon since we were twelve.

Eying me suspiciously, Jill noted, "You seem to have lots of girl friends."

My laugh sounded sad in my ears. "I have lots of girl friends, but never a girlfriend."

"Until now," Jill said quickly, kissing me on the cheek and darting into home room.

I stood stunned in the doorway until Miss Tomlinson finally nudged me.

"Senor Lanier, would you like to come into home room, or would you prefer to remain in the hall?"

"Uh, yes, I mean no, or, uh, yes, I would like to come into class, no, I don't want to stay in the hall."

She gestured toward my desk. "Then by all means, please come in and take your seat."

The look on Miss Tomlinson's face was one of patient amusement. I headed to my seat and noticed Jill looking at me with a smile like the cat who just ate the canary. I felt the blood rising in my face and did not look at Jill or Miss Tomlinson the whole home room period. Not an easy thing to accomplish as they were both rather pleasant to look at.

By the time Spanish Class started, I was over my embarrassment. I even managed to regain my wits by the time it ended. Jill asked me to walk her to her second period class. Even though it meant I would really have to hustle to make my own class, I did.

Walking along I asked her, in a shy, quiet voice, "Jill, did you mean it, about being my girlfriend, when you said it earlier?"

She bit at her lower lip and looked at me out of the corner of her eye. "Did you think I said it just to mess with your mind?"

I stopped short. Jill turned around and looked at me. "I really hope not."

She smiled an uncertain smile. "Why not?"

I took in a deep breath, held it a second or two, and plunged in. "Because I would really like to be your boyfriend."

Her eyes widened, and the uncertainty was gone from her smile. "Michael, are you asking me to go steady? Do boys still ask girls that?"

Getting the definite impression she liked the idea, I plowed on. "I guess, yes, I am. Jill, will you go steady with me?"

"Let me think about it." She took about two seconds to do so. "Yes, I'll go steady with you."

We arrived at her class. Jill kissed me on the cheek again, but this time it didn't fry my brain. As she disappeared into her class, I turned and made tracks towards mine, getting there just in time. It wasn't until I saw Hans waiting for me in class that it hit me. Having known her barely a day, I'd asked Jill to be my girlfriend. How had that happened?

Hans looked worried when I sat down next to him. "Michael, where have you been? You were almost tardy."

Still somewhat dazed by the realization that I had a girlfriend, I looked at him and blinked a couple times. "I walked Jill to her class."

Hans shook his head and chuckled. "Man, have you got it bad."

I grimaced and told him, "It's worse than you think."

His face grew serious. "What do you mean?"

"If you gentlemen are ready, I'd like to get started. We have a lot of material to cover today." Mr. Burton's glare clearly indicated his comment was directed at Hans and me.

Opening my notebook, I responded, "Yes, sir."

Hans looked at me as if blaming me for getting us in trouble. "We're sorry, Mr. Burton."

Hans had to wait until after Algebra 2 to find out what I meant. He didn't forget to ask as soon as we walked out of class. "What do you mean, 'It's worse than you think'?"

My face got all scrunched up like I was expecting to get hit. "I kind of asked Jill to go steady."

Hans shoulders slumped and his jaw dropped. "You've known Jill all of twenty-four hours, and you asked her to go steady?" Then a puzzled look came on his face. "Do people actually 'go steady' anymore?"

"I know it was a bit impetuous, but it seemed like the right thing to do. She said yes."

"Michael, this isn't like you. I think this girl bewitched you. You're under her spell." He couldn't help but laugh.

"Maybe I am, but it seems like a nice place to be from where I'm standing."

Hans patted me on the back. "I'll see you at lunch, Michael. I can hardly wait to hear what Beth and Rhiannon think of this development."

Hans turned down the hall to his next class, and I hustled to the rear building where the JROTC classroom was. While I'd been looking forward to lunch so I could see Jill, I suddenly wondered if I really wanted to be there at all.

Nine

When fourth period ended and lunch period arrived, I decided I wanted to see Jill more than I wanted to avoid Beth and Rhiannon, so I bravely made my way to the cafeteria. Jill was waiting for me outside the door. She gave me a quick hug as I walked up. "Hello there, brand new boyfriend of mine. How was the rest of your morning?"

Taking her hand as we walked in the door, I told her. "It went okay. I told Hans we're going steady."

Jill squeezed my hand. "Couldn't wait to share the good news, huh? Me either. I saw Beth on her way to band and just had to tell her."

A trickle of anxiety made its way out. "Oh yeah, what did she say?"

"She said she thought it was great," Jill reported enthusiastically, squeezing my hand again.

Relieved, I brought her hand up to my lips and kissed it gently. "Beth was right about that."

That was evidently the right thing to say as it earned me a hug right there in the lunch line. Over her shoulder I saw Hans come in with April. After getting our food we went to our table to wait for them. Beth and Wesley came in as we were sitting down. I hadn't seen Rhiannon.

"So you two are officially a couple," Beth said as she sat down.

Wes cast her an inquisitive glance. "They're a couple of what?"

Chuckling and shaking her head, Beth informed him. "Brat, they are officially boyfriend and girlfriend."

I nodded at Wes imperiously. "We are, yes, officially and for the record."

Jill didn't say anything; she just beamed at me. Hans laughed and Beth just shook her head. Rhiannon still hadn't come in.

Hans took a bite of his chicken patty sandwich and made a face. "Too dry," he said and picked up a mayonnaise packet. "So, Michael, are you going to the pier tonight?"

With a groan I set down my drink and gestured toward the stack of books next to my tray. "It depends on how long all this homework takes me. Mr. Burton has no problem assigning homework."

"No, he's very good at that."

"I heard that," Mr. Burton said as he walked by on his way to the teachers' table.

Beth stifled a laugh. "Now you've had it, you two. He'll double your work load."

Jill looked slightly baffled. "Where is this pier?"

Hans explained. "Well, there are three piers at Wrightsville Beach. There's Mercer's Pier near the north end. There's Crystal Pier in the middle of the island. Then there's Lumina Pier at the south end just up from the jetty. It's just down the street from Mike's house. Rhiannon's father owns it. When we say 'the pier,' we mean Lumina Pier."

A thoughtful if somewhat worried look crossed Jill's face. "Rhiannon's father owns it. How interesting. You guys spend a lot of time there?"

With a nod and a shrug Hans said, "It depends on the time of year. In the fall and spring we go a lot, but not so much in the winter, too cold."

Jill considered that for a moment. "What about summer? It seems like that would be the best time to go to a pier."

"Yeah," said Wes, "I would think so, too. My dad and I went up to the Iron Steamer Pier on Emerald Isle a lot in the summer."

Swallowing the last bite of my sandwich, I told them. "The thing about summer is neither Hans nor I are usually around much in the summer."

"Where do you go?" Jill asked.

"They leave town," Beth said with a trace of annoyance. "Hans leaves the country."

Befuddled, Jill asked, "What do you mean?"

"I spend every summer with my grandmother in Germany," Hans explained.

"And I spend most of every summer at Camp Riversail in Pamlico County. I used to go as a camper, but now I work as a counselor. And most summers I go spend a week with Hans and his grandmother."

Crumpling up his trash and stuffing it into his milk carton, Hans nodded. "Yeah, he usually does. Last summer my grandmother took us to Lake Geneva in Switzerland."

"That was cool," I recalled. "It is a beautiful place to sail."

"Sailing in Switzerland, is it that big a lake?" Jill asked. "I thought Switzerland was all mountains."

Beth made a disgusted sound and then laughed. "Mike would sail in a mud puddle if there was enough draft and wind."

"Lake Geneva is a large lake, over 45 miles long." Hans sounded like a geography teacher or maybe a tour guide. "Sailing is very popular on the lake."

"Maybe I can take you sailing sometime, Jill," I suggested.

Judging from the smile that lit up her face, she really liked the idea. "I've never been. It might be fun. Are you a good sailor?"

"Mike learned to sail before he could walk," Beth quipped. "He's pretty good."

"You've been sailing with him then?" Jill asked Beth with just a hint of hesitation.

Hans informed Jill, "If you want to hang out with Mike, you pretty much have to learn to sail. Otherwise, you'll never see him on weekends."

Jill looked at me with a smug grin. "I see. Then I'll just have to learn to sail."

I smiled back at her. "I'd love to teach you."

Lunch time was over and still no Rhiannon. On the way to Composition, I asked Beth if she knew what was up.

Beth was surprised I didn't know. "Rhiannon went to lunch with Sabrina. Didn't she tell you?"

Annoyed that Rhiannon hadn't told me, I replied, "No, she didn't. Who is Sabrina?"

Beth's expression was almost one of amusement. "She's a cheer-leader, a junior. Rhiannon has been moved up to the varsity squad because they didn't have enough girls. I guess she and Rhiannon really hit it off."

"Okay, but why didn't we see them in the cafeteria?"

Beth bowed her head to me in thanks for holding the door open before continuing. "Probably because Sabrina has a car and they went to Mickie D's or someplace. Why the twenty questions?"

"I don't know. When we got to school this morning, she hurried off and I haven't seen her since. I guess I was a little worried when she didn't show up for lunch."

"Mm, hm," Beth murmured with a satisfied smirk. "Were you worried she might be having lunch with some guy?"

"Why would that worry me?" I wasn't about to admit the thought had crossed my mind, leaving a slight sting when it did. "I think it'd be great if she met a guy." What was that funny hitch in my voice? I would be happy for Rhiannon, wouldn't I?

Much to my chagrin, Beth caught it too. "Oh, yeah, Michael, I'm sure you'd be happy as a clam if Rhiannon had a boyfriend."

Whether I would be or not was beside the point now that Jill and I were together. "Of course I would. After all, I've got a girlfriend. Besides, Rhiannon has made it quite clear I am not her type."

Beth's expression indicated she was not convinced. "That you've completely reconciled yourself to that is abundantly clear."

"It's a moot point anyway, isn't it? She didn't go to lunch with some guy, she went with Sabrina. She could have at least told me."

"Michael, I am so glad you have completely put the thought of you and Rhiannon as a couple out of your mind." Beth's voice dripped with sarcasm.

"Leave it alone, Beth. I'm with Jill now."

We were almost late for Miss Preston's class. Was Beth right? I had reconciled myself to the idea Rhiannon and I were never going to happen. She was one of my best friends but would never be my girlfriend. Jill was my girlfriend. It happened kind of fast, sure, but so what? I liked her, she liked me, and she was a knockout. We didn't really know each other, but wasn't the mystery supposed to be part of the magic? I told myself firmly that it was.

Composition class went by in a blur, and I almost forgot to go to the gym instead of Social Studies seventh period. On away-game days athletes missed seventh period so they could get ready for and travel to their games. That year Laney only had a varsity soccer team, so Hans and I could say we made varsity our sophomore year.

Everyone who went out for soccer at Laney made varsity. There were only fourteen of us. We prayed no one would get hurt.

When the football team went to an away game, the cheerleaders went with them. Not so for us soccer players. They didn't cheer for us at home games either. Cheering was reserved for football and basketball.

With only fourteen of us to play, it was a sure bet everyone would get game time. As the last to show up for summer practice, I would start this first game against North Brunswick on the bench. Coach explained to me that it wasn't a reflection of my skill, though it may have been; rather, it was because he thought the guys who had been to the most practices should get the first chance to play. I wasn't going to argue because I agreed completely.

The game turned out to be a losing effort but not for lack of trying on our part. North Brunswick only beat us by one goal, 2 to 1. They didn't score the winning goal until the last two minutes. Coach was pretty proud of us. I played the last fifteen minutes of the second half after one of the midfielders left the game with a wicked cramp.

Dad was waiting to take Hans and me home when we got back to Laney. "How was the game?"

A dejected Hans replied simply, "We lost."

I was a little more positive about the outcome. "We did a lot better than expected, and Hans scored."

Glancing over his shoulder, Dad said, "Great, good for you, Hans. What was the final score?"

Dad's praise seemed to lift Hans' spirits a little. "Two to one. We had tied it up at the beginning of the second half, but they scored with two minutes left."

"I got to play the last fifteen minutes," I said proudly. Then with a little more humility, I revealed why. "Jay got a bad cramp."

"It sounds like you made a good showing, all in all."

"I suppose we did," Hans reluctantly admitted. "Still, I would have enjoyed it more if we'd won."

We dropped Hans off at his house in Long Leaf Acres, a subdivision about five miles up Eastwood Road from the beach. Hans and I both decided we wouldn't make it to the pier as it was already late and we had plenty of homework. Between Algebra, Chemistry, and Composition, it promised to be a long night. Disappointed as I was that Hans and I wouldn't get to hang out at the pier, I found I was more upset about not getting to see Rhiannon. She almost always worked the snack bar in the evenings. Shrugging to myself, I figured I would see her on the bus in the morning.

I wasn't able to get right to my homework when I got home. Mom had a message for me to call some girl named Jill. "Is she the young lady in your homeroom you mentioned meeting yesterday?"

I may have blushed just a little. "Yes, ma'am, she's that young lady."

Mom set her magazine on her lap and scrutinized me carefully. "Did she reply in the affirmative regarding the game tomorrow night?" My mother always talked like that. She went to one of those fancy New England girls' colleges.

Dad laughed as he sat down in his recliner. "What your mother means, Michael, is did the girl's parents say 'yes?'" Dad often felt like he had to translate for my mother. He earned his college degree in night school after getting out of the Navy.

Giving my father a withering look, Mom informed him, "Michael knows perfectly well what I meant, Owen, thank you very much. Michael, did she?"

"Yes, ma'am, she did, with the caveat that I meet her father when he drops her off at the game."

Mom pursed her lips, nodded, and picked up her magazine. "A perfectly reasonable request, if you ask me."

"I thought so."

I went up to my room to call Jill. "Hello?" a male voice answered.

Slightly nervous, I said, "Hello, sir. This is Mike Lanier. I'm returning Jill's call. I hope I'm not calling too late."

"Not at all, Mike, Jill's been waiting for your call." He sounded friendly enough. "This is Jill's dad by the way."

"It's very nice to speak to you, sir. I'm looking forward to meeting you tomorrow." I spoke in my most respectful and formal manner.

"And I'm looking forward to meeting you, but please, call me Ellis. I'll get Jill."

"Hi, Mike," Jill said as she came on the phone. She sounded pleased I'd called.

"Hi, I got your message."

"I was just wondering how the game went."

That disappointed me for some reason; if it was the only reason she'd called. "We lost two to one, but we did better than anyone thought we'd do. Hans scored our only goal."

"All right, Hans!" Jill sounded genuinely enthused. "Did you get to play?"

"I played the last fifteen minutes of the second half, after Jay got a cramp." I knew I didn't sound nearly as enthused as she had. "I got a few touches, nothing much."

"What does 'a few touches' mean?"

"It's soccer talk for I got to kick the ball."

"Oh." Her tone changed just slightly when she asked, "Did you guys get to go to the pier?"

"No, it got to be too late, and I've still got a ton of homework."

I could almost see her nod sympathetically. "Then I should probably let you go so you can get to work."

"I can talk for a little while," I said quickly, not wanting her to think I was trying to rush her off the phone.

"No, I'd better go. I've still got some homework myself."

"Okay, I'll see you tomorrow."

My clock showed it was near midnight when I finally got my homework done. It was going to be tough getting up in the morning. I should have fallen asleep thinking about my date with Jill the next night. Instead, I fell asleep wondering what was going on with Rhiannon.

Ten

The next morning at the bus stop I was in for a surprise. I kept checking my watch and looking over towards her house next to the pier, but no Rhiannon. That was really weird. Rhiannon and I had ridden together on one bus or another since first grade. Sure, there were times when one of us was sick or something, but since at least third grade we'd always called and told each other when we'd be out. The bus came and still no Rhiannon. I rode to school alone in our seat.

Arriving at school, I went and found Hans. I told him Rhiannon hadn't shown up at the bus stop and asked if he'd seen her at school.

Hans looked puzzled, too. "No Michael, I haven't seen her this morning. Maybe she's sick."

I shook my head in exasperation. "She would've called, or her mom would. Something's going on."

Giving me a look that clearly meant he thought I was making too much of it, Hans asked, "What do you think is going on?"

Maybe I was making too much of it, but it bugged me. "That's just it, I don't know. But it isn't like her to leave me in the dark."

"What're you two talking about?" Beth asked as she walked up.

Hans pointed at me and said, "Michael is worried about Rhiannon."

Beth looked perplexed. "Why?"

"She didn't ride the bus this morning," I said.

Beth looked at me like I was worried over nothing. "She probably caught a ride with Sabrina. Sabrina lives in Windemere. It wouldn't be far out of her way to drive to the beach to pick up Rhiannon."

"That is a possibility," Hans said, hoping to reassure me.

If it was the explanation, it still grated on me that Rhiannon hadn't said anything to me about it. "But why wouldn't she tell me?"

"Geez, Mike, if I didn't know better I'd say you were jealous," Beth quipped in a teasing tone. "Are you jealous?"

Tilting my head and rolling my eyes, I gave her a sharp look. "No, of course not, I'm just surprised and a little hurt. It's not like her to just shut me out and leave me in the dark."

"Who's shutting you out and leaving you in the dark, baby?" Jill asked as she arrived on the scene.

Beth saw an opportunity to not-so-subtly remind me what was what. "Rhiannon changed her schedule and didn't check with Big Brother here. Now he's having a conniption."

Coming to my defense, Hans interjected. "That's a bit overstated, Beth. Michael's just worried about this sudden change in Rhiannon. I must admit, I'm a bit surprised by it myself."

Jill shrugged and suggested innocently, "Then why don't you go over to the student parking lot and ask her?"

My head snapped around a little too quickly. "Is that where she is?"

Seeing my reaction, Jill's shoulders slumped. "She was a minute ago when my dad dropped me off." She turned from me and looked at the ground. Absorbed in my own thoughts, I missed Jill's reaction to my response to her news about Rhiannon's whereabouts.

"You don't have time now, the bell's about to ring," Beth noted.

Realizing Beth was right about the time, I turned to Jill and abruptly changed the subject. "I was sure happy to get your message from my mom last night. I wanted to call when I got home from the game but thought it'd be too late."

Evidently I once again stumbled on the right thing to say as the concerned furrow beginning to crease her brow disappeared. She smiled and took my arm. "I really wanted to know how the game turned out. I wanted to know if my favorite player had played well."

Hans made a slight bow in her direction. "Thank you for thinking of me, Jill. I actually did score a goal."

Jill looked at him and tried to figure out if he was kidding or had misunderstood. I stifled a laugh and set him straight. "Um, old buddy, I think she meant me."

"Of course I meant you, Mike, but Hans, congratulations on your goal." She pulled me closer and put her head on my shoulder. "Really, I just didn't want to wait until this morning to talk to you."

Her head against my shoulder felt rather nice. "I'm glad you didn't." We walked the rest of the way to home room holding hands. Rhiannon was down the hall by Mrs. Nadeau's door, but I decided if she wanted to keep me at arm's length for some reason I would accommodate her. I didn't see her turn to watch Jill and me go through into class.

At lunch Rhiannon came in with Sabrina, but they didn't come and sit with us. Instead they went to the "cheerleader" table. I looked up and waved. Either Rhiannon didn't see me or wanted not to see me. Jill looked a little annoyed that I was annoyed Rhiannon didn't acknowledge me. She took my hand and led me to the little courtyard outside the cafeteria. "Mike, I've got to ask this. Are you in love with Rhiannon?"

Hesitation here could have been deadly, the truth even worse. I prevaricated. "It's not like that, sweetheart. Rhiannon and I have been friends our whole lives. Now suddenly she acts like I don't exist. Friends don't treat friends like that. I'd be just as upset if it were Hans." Okay, maybe not quite as upset, but Jill didn't need to know that.

Jill took my chin in her hand and tilted my head down until she was looking me right in the eye. "Mike, we've only known each other a few days, but I really like you. I liked you right off. I think we can have a lot of fun together but not if you're carrying a torch for Rhiannon."

"Jill, the only 'torch' I'm carrying right now is for you," I said, trying hard to make her believe it.

"Okay." Then she added, "I'm sorry."

Her apology was unexpected. "Sorry, for what, babe?"

"Sorry for not understanding. She's your friend and you're worried about her. I can understand that. I guess part of what I like about you so much is your loyalty to your friends." Putting her arms around me, she gave me a hug. I returned the gesture, and as we pulled apart bent my face to hers and we shared our first on-the-mouth kiss.

Returning to our seats, we were greeted by the applause of our table mates. They'd seen the whole thing. Jill turned a most interesting shade of red. Beth wasn't clapping, but over her shoulder I saw Rhiannon smiling at me. Maybe everything was not as it seemed.

Jill and I shared another quick kiss at the end of lunch before heading to our classes. Rhiannon caught up with me on my way to Composition. "I can't talk long, Bro, or I'll be late. I just wanted to say way to go." Rhiannon called me "Bro" when she wanted to remind me we were too much like brother and sister to go out together.

"Rhiannon, wait..." I called to her retreating back. What in the world was going on? I turned back toward class only to bump smack into Beth.

"Quite a show you and Jill put on, Michael. At least Rhiannon seems happy for you."

Her indignant tone surprised me. "Green is an ugly color on you, Elisabeth."

"Jealous, me, of what?"

"You're right; you have nothing to be jealous of. You have a boyfriend and he's not me."

Beth recoiled from the ice in my voice. "No," she said quietly, "he's not you, Michael."

Seeing the hurt look on her face, I felt like a jerk. "Beth, I'm sorry, that was uncalled for."

With a weak smile Beth looked up at me. "Michael, can I tell you something? I mean something super secret."

Not knowing what sort of secret she might have in mind to share, I still let her know she could share it with me. "You know you can, Beth. You're my friend and you know I don't make friends lightly."

Her smile brightened a little. "I know. It's part of what I love about you. I do love you Michael, but I'm not in love with you. Do you know what I mean?"

I started to say I was all too painfully aware of what she meant but realized it wasn't the time for sarcasm. Besides, I wouldn't be talking about her, but she wouldn't know that. Instead I swallowed hard. "Yes, Beth, I know."

"And I am glad you and Jill are going out, really. It's just, how can I say this? You were always my ace in the hole, Michael. If things didn't work out with Greg, I told myself you'd always be there for me. In the back of my mind I was always glad you didn't have a girlfriend." She paused to take a breath. "God, I'm not making any sense."

"Beth, I think I understand, and it's okay. I'm still your friend, and I'll still catch you when you fall, but now there are two of us to help you get back on your feet." That wasn't what she meant and I knew it, but I felt like I needed to say something.

"You and Jill, you mean." Neither her face nor voice showed any enthusiasm for the idea.

Smiling what I hoped was a gentle, sympathetic smile I said, "Yeah, me and Jill. She really would like to be your friend."

Beth thought about that for a moment. "Well, since you seem to be bound and determined to keep her around, I guess I can give her a chance."

"That's all that I ask."

Miss Preston was waiting impatiently for us at her door. Evidently we never heard the tardy bell. "I'm going to let it go this time, you two, but in the future save your romancing for outside of class time."

Beth and I smiled knowingly at each other and promised we would.

The rest of the day passed without incident, thank goodness. Jill loaned me her notes from Social Studies during home room, so I wasn't completely clueless during seventh period. Jill and I held hands as we left class. There was no soccer practice on Friday. As I turned to walk back to the bus lot, she tugged me toward the front of the school.

"Jill, my bus is back there. You don't want me to miss it, do you?"

A mischievous grin flickered across her face. "As a matter of fact, I do. My dad's picking us up."

Alarm bells started going off in my mind. "He's picking us up?"

Jill tugged eagerly at my arm. "Yup, come on."

Succumbing to the inevitable, I let her lead me to the front of the school. A VW Bus was parked there with a ponytailed gentleman at the wheel. He climbed out when he saw us.

Jill was practically dancing as we approached the van. "Daddy, meet Mike Lanier. Mike, this is my dad, Ellis Jonas."

"It's a pleasure to meet you, sir," I said, extending my hand.

Her father took my hand in a firm grip. "Good to meet you in person, Mike. What's with the 'sir' stuff, I thought we agreed on the phone you'd call me Ellis."

"Yes, sir…I mean okay, Ellis. Sorry, habit. I wasn't expecting to meet you until tonight."

"I know, but I thought since I was picking Jillian up anyway, this would give us a chance to talk, get to know each other, and maybe I could meet at least one of your folks when we get to your house."

Meeting my folks, I realized, was the real reason for the offer of a ride home. "You may get to meet them both. Dad works out of the house, and Mom is usually home, too."

Ellis motioned for us to get in the van. Jill sat in back and pointed me toward the front passenger seat. While we were waiting in line for our chance to pull out onto College Road, Ellis asked, "What does your father do that he gets to work from home?"

"He's kind of a financial manager. He tracks portfolios for several business investments and charitable foundations, those kinds of things." What I left out was that the investments were all mine, or mine through the trust, and all the charitable foundations had been set up at my request. Such information was not public knowledge. Very few of my friends even knew much about it. Rhiannon and Hans had some idea. Beth knew I was well off, or that my family was. The others in our circle knew I lived in a waterfront house on the sound so assumed my family must have money. I didn't think any of that would make appropriate conversation just then.

Looking left and right at the traffic, Ellis realized we would be sitting there a while. "Very interesting. Me, I'm a nuclear scientist.

Actually, I'm a nuclear engineer at General Electric. That's how we wound up here in Wilmington."

I learned a lot about Ellis and his family on that ride. For instance, I learned Jill's birthday was January 28, that her mother, Cierra, was an artist, and her grandmother on her mother's side owned an art gallery in Asheville. I learned Ellis graduated from MIT with a PhD in something very technical involving producing nuclear reactor fuel after earning his undergraduate and master's degrees at North Carolina State. I learned he and Jill's mom had been together almost twenty years but had not yet married. And I learned about Oliver, though I think that was a slip on Ellis' part. Oliver was Jill's boyfriend back in Asheville. She assured me he was her very ex-boyfriend.

To get all this told, Ellis actually drove to the North End of Wrightsville Beach and then to the South End before turning down our little street and pulling up to my house. My dad was sitting out on the deck reading the Wall Street Journal when he heard the van pull up and came around to see who was pulling in.

Seeing him come down the stairs as I climbed from the van, I called out, "Hi, Dad, there are some people here I'd like you to meet."

Dad surveyed us from the top of the stairs and smiled. "Okay, Mike, ask them to come on up."

Jill and Ellis got out of the van and followed me up the steps. "Dad, I'd like to introduce Ellis Jonas and his daughter Jill. This is my dad, Owen Lanier."

Dad took Ellis' outstretched hand. "It's a pleasure to meet you Mr. Jonas. You too, young lady."

"Please, Mr. Lanier, call me Ellis," Ellis said, noting the strength of my Dad's handshake. I don't think he expected a financial manager to have such a grip.

"Only if you will call me Owen." My dad was never one to stand much on formality.

This apparently pleased Jill's dad. "Agreed."

Jill stepped up to my Dad and held out her hand. "What should I call you, Mr. Lanier?"

Dad took her hand. "Most of Michael's friends call me Mr. L. Will that work for you?" He seemed a bit puzzled by the question.

"OK, Mr. L," Jill said happily.

Dad indicated they should precede us into the house, and I pulled him aside. "Mr. L., no one calls you Mr. L. Where did that come from?"

Dad shrugged. "I don't know. I guess the question caught me off guard. Why would she ask a question like that?"

I answered with a shrug of my own. "She probably asked because her dad told me to call him Ellis."

"I see. Should I let her call me Owen? I'm not comfortable with that."

I laughed. "It looks to me like you're stuck being Mr. L. Should I tell my other friends to start calling you that?"

"Why not? I think I like it," he said after a moment's thought. "Now, shouldn't we follow your guests inside?"

We followed my guests inside to discover Ellis and Jill had introduced themselves to my mother and to Malori my three-and-a-half-year-old sister. Mom and Ellis were chatting amiably.

My mom looked up and smiled a not-so-sincere smile at me as we walked in. "Michael, it is so nice of you to join us. Your guests took it upon themselves to make the introductions. You were quite right, son; Jill is a lovely young lady."

Being used to my mother's quirky sense of humor, I knew she wasn't really upset. "I'm glad you agree, Mom. May I take Jill on a tour of the house while you, Dad, and her father trade embarrassing childhood stories about us?"

Mom's eyes widened as if shocked. "I am sorry, Mr. Jonas, his father and I did not know we were raising such a precocious child."

She said this with such perfect seriousness that Jill's jaw dropped and Ellis stood there with a stunned expression on his face. Then Mom smiled, Dad started laughing, and I just shook my head.

"You will have to pardon my wife's sense of humor," Dad said between laughs.

Ellis caught on quickly. "Oh, I understand completely. We have to keep Jillian here away from polite company too."

Jill looked scandalized. "Dad, I thought that was a family secret." Try as she might, she couldn't say it with a straight face and broke down laughing herself.

I smiled patiently and waited for everyone to collect themselves. "If everyone is quite through, I will now take Jill on the nickel tour."

Mom indicated Ellis should join Dad and her at the table and waved the two of us on our way. I showed Jill through the house, ending up in my loft.

Jill was amazed. "This whole floor of the house is yours?"

"It was my grandfather's. When he passed away I moved up here."

Jill walked out onto the sundeck. "What a great view. It's not the mountains, but it's still a great view."

I walked out beside her and put my arm around her. "I come out here every morning to work out and never get tired of seeing it."

Stretching out over the railing to take in as much of the view as she could, Jill sighed contentedly. "You are so lucky."

"I know," I said turning her toward me. Our kiss was interrupted by my dad hollering up the stairs.

"Say, Mike, why don't you take Jill out to the dock and show her your boat?"

I had to try twice to find my voice. "Okay, Dad."

Jill ran a finger down my nose and then poked my chin. "Too bad, I kind of liked what we were doing."

"Dad probably guessed what we were doing. That's why he suggested we go outside."

We went downstairs and down the dock to my sailboat, Hey 19, a West White Potter 19-footer I named after the Steely Dan song. It was a nice little boat with a small cabin you could crawl into but couldn't stand up in if you were more than five feet tall.

"Nice boat," Jill remarked. "Is it hard to sail?"

"No, it's actually pretty easy. Maybe I can teach you?"

"I'd like that."

As we sat in the cockpit, I started explaining what was what. Too soon Ellis and my dad came looking for us. It was time for Ellis and Jill to get going.

Reaching down to help her up to the dock, Ellis said, "Jill, Michael's dad has offered to pick you up for the game and drop you off after y'all have some fun at Mikey's. Sound okay to you?"

Jill stepped carefully from the boat to the dock. "Sounds good to me, Dad. Thanks, Mr. L."

"Yeah, Dad, thanks," I added. We walked with them to the van and saw them on their way. Then I told Dad I was going for a quick ride up to the pier before coming back to get ready for the game.

I didn't go to the pier but to the Angevin's house next door. Rhiannon was home. She wouldn't be working that night since she would be cheering at the game.

Eleven

"Michael, what are you doing here?" a surprised Rhiannon asked when she answered the door.

Now that I was there, I wasn't sure what I wanted to say. I shuffled my feet for a second. "Well, I figured you would be so busy cheering at the game we wouldn't get a chance to talk. Not knowing if you were going to Mikey's after the game, I figured if I wanted to talk to you I better get myself over here and talk to you."

She seemed taken aback. "Wow, okay, what do you want to talk about?"

I bit my lip as if I couldn't quite remember. "Let me think, I know there was something." After looking at the door for a couple seconds as if trying to recall what I wanted to talk about, I snapped my fingers. "Oh, I remember. How come you've been avoiding me for the last two days?"

Rhiannon breathed a deep sigh and checked her watch. "Let's go for a quick walk."

"Okay."

We walked up the path between her house and the pier until we reached the beach. The waves lapped the shore just short of wetting our shoes. We walked along talking for a time. Finally

Rhiannon stopped and turned to me. "How're you and Jill gettin' along, everything going okay?"

That wasn't the subject I'd come to discuss, but if Rhiannon wanted to talk about it, then I'd tell her. "Jill and I are doing great. In fact, she and her dad came to meet my parents after school today. While they were busy comparing notes, Jill and I were necking in my room, until my dad interrupted." It was childish and petty, but I hoped it stung her at least a little.

"Really," Rhiannon said with an uncomfortable laugh in her voice. "I'm glad to hear it."

My temper almost got the better of me, almost. "Well, I don't know if I'm glad you're glad. Rhiannon, please tell me what's going on?"

"I'm gay," Rhiannon said. No preamble, no setting me up for it, she just came out and said it. I looked around to see if someone else might have said it. Then I looked at her. Then I looked out to sea. Then I looked at her again. I could see by the look on her face she was quite serious.

"That explains a lot." It never entered my mind to ask if she was sure.

My response to her revelation clearly irritated her. "What does that mean?"

"It explains how you've been able to resist my ample charm and good looks all these years." Her expression showed my attempt at humor didn't work. "It explains why I'm not your type," I said bitterly, my voice cracking. I didn't know whether to laugh or cry. I don't think she did either.

"Michael, I never meant to hurt you. The last thing in the world I want to do is hurt you. I do love you, Michael. It's just that I can never be in love with you. Do you understand?" Rhiannon was practically begging.

"Oh, I understand. Actually, I'm kind of getting used to it. You're the second female friend who's said it to me today." I was agitated, aggravated, angry, confused and hurting.

Rhiannon looked shocked. "Don't tell me Jill…"

I laughed a humorless laugh. "It was Beth, Rhiannon. It was Beth."

"Beth!?" She reached up and took my face none too gently between her hands. "Beth told you she loves you but she's not in love with you?"

Twisting my head out of her grasp, I said, "Yeah, it must be screw with Mike's heart day."

"Poor Michael." Rhiannon's unsympathetic tone didn't match her words. "You want to know why I avoided you these last two days?"

Did I want to know? How could she even ask? "Why? Please tell me why!"

"To give you and Jill room." Rhiannon said it as if it were the most reasonable explanation in the world.

It was also the last thing I expected. "Room for what?"

Rhiannon looked at me the way a frustrated teacher looks at difficult student. "Room to fall for each other without me distracting you or worrying her. I'm not blind, Michael. Every time you looked at her or she moved closer to you, you looked at me. Jill noticed that, Mike."

I didn't know what to say. She was right. I loved Rhiannon. I might have liked Jill. I did like Jill. I liked Jill a lot. But I loved Rhiannon. And Rhiannon could never love me back, not with the same kind of love. My heart was breaking. Tears filled my eyes.

"My dear Michael, I can't remember a time when my friend Mike wasn't there for me. Please don't hate me." Rhiannon was crying now, too. "I couldn't bear that. Please Michael, I'm begging you, please tell me you can forgive me and we can still be friends. Please."

I looked into her eyes and saw the fear there. What could I do? My Rhiannon needed me. My friend Rhiannon needed her friend Mike, more than Mike needed a girlfriend named Rhiannon. I built a wall around the part of my heart that was in love with Rhiannon and reached out to my friend.

"I could never hate you, Rhiannon. You're the best friend I've ever had. There's nothing to forgive. You never made me any promises or led me on. I was the one who couldn't see what was right there in front of me. I love you, Rhiannon. Maybe I can't be in love with you, but I will always love you."

I don't know how long we stood there on the beach with me holding her for all I was worth because I knew that as soon as I let go, I was letting go of more than that embrace; I was letting go of a dream I had held onto for so long.

Rhiannon swallowed hard and wiped her eyes with the back of her hand. "Thank you, Michael. If I could make things different, I would."

"Things will be what things will be."

She glanced at her watch and then towards her house. "We'd probably better get back."

"Yeah, I guess so." And somehow that was it, one chapter closed. I felt a little numb, like a callus had grown inside somewhere. It had hurt for a quick, painful moment, but I knew I was going to be all right. "You know, Rhiannon, I was just thinking, this could be kind of interesting."

"How so?"

"Well, I've never had a best friend who's a lesbian before. This'll be a whole new adventure."

"You, Michael, you are a brat." But when she said it she laughed, and by the time we got to her house and I got on my bike, we were both smiling. Things would never be the same, but at least we'd still be friends.

Twelve

I got home in plenty of time to change and clean up for the game. In a funny way I felt lighter somehow. Looking forward to seeing Jill, I wondered if she would notice anything different about me.

Dad and I found Jill's house in Porter's Neck with no trouble. Ellis gave Dad precise directions. Dad insisted on walking to the door with me, ostensibly to meet Jill's mom. Ellis answered the door.

"Come in, come in. Jill will be ready in a minute. I'd like you two to meet Jill's mom." Ellis turned towards the back of the house and called out. "Cierra, Jill's young man is here, with his father."

As Jill's mother walked out, Dad and I caught our breath. Even with her golden-blond hair pulled up, and wearing a painter's smock that did nothing to disguise her tall, shapely figure, Cierra was stunning. There was no other word for it. It was obvious where Jill got her good looks.

Smoothing her smock as she approached, she looked up and smiled. "Sorry I'm such a mess. I was working on my latest project. I'm Cierra."

Dad bowed his head toward her. "No need to apologize. It's a pleasure to meet you."

Trying hard not to stare, I followed my Dad's lead. "Yes, ma'am, it is a pleasure."

Cierra chuckled delightfully. "None of this ma'am stuff, Mike, you'll make me feel like an old lady."

Distressed by the thought, I hurriedly said, "I wouldn't want to do that."

She reached out and brushed her nails lightly against my cheek. "Good, then please call me Cierra."

"Oh, hi, Mike, Mr. L, I'm ready to go," Jill called out as she came down the hall. Her hair was pulled back in a pony tail, and she wore blue jeans and a casual white blouse. A blue windbreaker was slung over her arm. She looked every bit as pretty as her mother.

Ellis gave Jill a quick hug. "Have a good time tonight, honey. Be back by dawn."

Cierra gave him a sharp look. He returned it with an innocent who me expression. Smiling politely, she turned to me. "Perhaps just a bit earlier than that, Mike. Jill should be home by midnight, or she turns into a pumpkin."

Jill rolled her eyes and made this funny little sound as she drew in a breath. "Cinderella's carriage turned into a pumpkin, Mom, not Cinderella."

Trying to keep a straight face, I assured Cierra we would have Jill home on time.

"Dear, it is Friday night, and it's a long way out here from the beach. Perhaps if they leave the club at midnight and come straight here," Ellis suggested with a conspiratorial wink in my direction.

Cierra gave this a moment's thought. Turning to my dad, she asked, "Would that be a problem, Owen?"

"No, that would actually work out better."

Ellis looked satisfied they had taken his suggestion. "Then it's settled. You kids have a good time."

I took Jill's hand, and we walked out to the Suburban where I held the door for her like a real gentleman. Dad sat up front, but I walked around to the other side and got in back next to Jill. "Are monsieur and mademoiselle ready to go?" Dad asked with a corny French accent.

Playing along with him, I replied, "Mes oui, Gaston, you may proceed."

Jill chuckled and rolled her eyes. "You two are something."

Since I thought it might come up during the night, I figured I'd be preemptive and tell Jill I'd talked to Rhiannon. Jill didn't act jealous the way I'd feared she might. She seemed more curious than anything. "Did she tell you why she was acting so mysterious?"

"She said she did it to give us room. She thought because she and I'd been friends for so long, you and I might have trouble connecting if she were always around."

Jill reached over and took my hand. "Your friend Rhiannon is very astute. Being that it made both of us think about her more instead of less, I don't think it worked out like she expected. But it did work out, didn't it?"

I squeezed her hand and lifted it briefly to my lips. "It did, because here we are on our first date, just the two of us."

"Well, except for your dad." Jill laughed.

I laughed too. "Yeah, except for him."

Then Jill leaned over and kissed me on the cheek. Dad pretended not to notice.

Hans and April were waiting for us at the gate. They'd ride with us to Mikey's and then we'd take them home. Dad was going to stay at the game and work in the concession stand. The school had received an anonymous donation to build a first-class concession stand at the football field. What would a Friday night game be without hot dogs, fries, and a Coke? Very hungry, that's what. None of us had eaten supper as we were counting on some of those hot dogs.

Hans was standing by the ticket booth with his hands on his hips and a look of disapproval on his face. "It's about time you got here, Michael. We've been waiting for hours."

April rolled her eyes and shook her head. "Minutes must count as hours in Germany. We just got dropped off ourselves."

A stricken look replaced Hans' look of indignation. "Alas, betrayed by my true love."

Hans and I bought the tickets while the girls chatted. Once we were inside, the inevitable occurred. "April, would you help me find the little girls' room?" Jill asked.

"I was just thinking of locating it myself."

"Girls always go in pairs; what's the story with that?" Hans asked rhetorically.

Shrugging to show I had no answer, I told the girls, "We'll wait for you over by the concession stand."

Other volunteers had arrived earlier to get things set up, and the hot dogs were already cooking. Dad was elected to handle the money end of things.

We stood there scanning the crowd for a while before Hans brought up something that was on his mind. "So, things are good with you and Jill?"

Puzzled by his cautious tone, I turned to see a somewhat concerned look on his face. "They couldn't be better. Why, what have you heard?"

He bit his lower lip and furrowed his brow. It looked as if he was trying to decide how much to say. "Mom went fishing early today. She saw you and Rhiannon on the beach together." He hesitated and rubbed his hand over his head before adding, "She said it looked like you were both crying."

I looked past him back towards the gate. "What are the odds?"

Hans reached out and put his hand on my shoulder. "Want to tell me what happened?"

So I told him most of it, enough of it. If Rhiannon wanted him to know more, she could tell him.

When I was finished, he let out a big sigh. "Michael, that's pretty heavy."

I frowned and nodded. "It was. Now the weight has lifted."

With all the commotion around us, I wasn't aware the girls had returned until Jill asked, "What weight has lifted?"

Startled, I turned just as she walked up and put her arms around me. Thinking quickly to distract her, I said, "The heaviness that weighed on my heart while I pined for you here 'ere you were there."

She laughed and kissed me. "You're a nut, but that was sweet." Turning to April she asked, "Eats or seats first?"

"I'm starving," April said. Taking Hans by the arm, she pulled him toward the concession stand. "Let's eat."

Jill nodded her agreement. "I'm with April. Let's check out the menu."

"They have hot dogs with or without chili, fries with or without cheese, soda, and a variety of candy bars and chips." They all stopped and looked at me. "What, they held the meeting to decide what to offer at my house."

We got hot dogs, fries, and drinks then found seats in the bleachers close to the forty-yard line. The cheerleaders were warming up and stretching. Rhiannon looked up, saw us, smiled, and waved. We all waved back. I checked carefully. Was that a little twinge? Maybe, or maybe I was just hungry.

We ate our hot dogs. The marching band came out and played. We saw Beth, but if she saw us she didn't let on. The team was introduced as they ran through a paper banner held aloft by the cheerleaders. Coins flipped, whistles blew, the ball was kicked, and Buccaneer football was underway. We cheered for the good plays, fussed at the bad calls, and generally enjoyed ourselves very much. When the final whistle sounded, much to everyone's surprise, we'd won the game.

The bleachers cleared out slowly, and eventually we met up with the gang by the gate. Wesley arrived first. He'd been part of the NJROTC Color Guard. Beth was a close second.

Finally Rhiannon walked up with Sabrina and a few other cheerleaders. "Hi, guys. I'll meet you there, okay? I'm riding with Sabrina." Amidst a chorus of "Okay, see you there," I threw Rhiannon an inquisitive look. The look she gave me in reply said, "Wouldn't you like to know?" but answered my question.

Thirteen

Beth sat up front with Dad. Jill and I squeezed into the third seat, while Wesley, Hans, and April took up the second seat. In short order we were seated in a corner table at Mikey's enjoying sodas, snacks, and music. Greg was already there waiting for Beth. He looked a little perturbed when we walked in looking like three couples. I hoped he was perturbed. I never liked him much anyway. Rhiannon and Sabrina came in a few minutes later and took a seat at the table next to ours.

Rhiannon looked a little nervous, yet excited at the same time. "Do you guys all know Sabrina?"

There were the usual replies of "seen you around school, never really met," and the like as everyone else at the table introduced themselves to Rhiannon's friend.

I hadn't said anything, leaving it up to Rhiannon to introduce me to Sabrina. "The tall, silent one there by Jill is my best friend Michael. Jill and Michael are now a couple, and I'm so happy for them." Was I the only one who thought she sounded a bit sarcastic?

I forced a smile and bowed my head toward Rhiannon's friend. "It's nice to meet you, Sabrina. I hope you'll enjoy being part of our circle."

Jill touched my arm and looked at me in a way that warmed me, a way that told me she understood what hadn't been said. "I'm new to this bunch of crazies too, Sabrina. Once you get to know them, you'll be glad you did." Then she kind of hugged my arm and kissed my cheek. "I am."

I put my arm around her, and she put her head on my shoulder while looking up into my eyes. I kissed her lightly on the forehead. Then I looked at Sabrina and Rhiannon. Sabrina was smiling shyly, but Rhiannon was looking at Jill and me like she'd just tasted something sour.

At that moment I wondered if I would be able to love Rhiannon without being in love with her. I looked back down at Jill, and she was gazing at me with an unsuspecting smile. What I felt for Jill might not be love, but it sure felt good. I kissed her again and asked her to dance.

When we returned to the table, I noticed another young lady had joined our group. She was sitting next to Wesley, and he was busy introducing her. "Everyone, this is Alyssa. Alyssa, this is everybody."

Alyssa had light brown hair, brown eyes, and wore those little spectacle-type gold-rimmed glasses. A pleasing smile lit up her face. "Hi, everybody, it's nice to meet you. Please call me Allie."

Once again we all introduced ourselves. By now we'd pushed two tables together to accommodate everyone. Our little circle was growing.

Wesley held Alyssa's chair for her and then sat down. "Allie is in my Geometry class. I got lucky, and Mr. Shumaker assigned me to the seat right behind hers."

Allie bopped him lightly on the arm. "I'm the lucky one. I don't get Geometry at all, but Wes is really good at it."

"I do okay." Wes seemed embarrassed by her praise.

"False modesty does not become you, Wesley," I said officiously.

Beth's laugh was more of a snort. "And Michael should know; he doesn't have a modest bone in his body."

Clutching my hand to my chest as if wounded, I assumed a pained expression. "Ah, Beth, you cut me deep." Everyone laughed.

Sabrina returned from the soda bar with refills for her and Rhiannon. "Did you guys know all drinks are half-price tonight for Laney students?"

"That's because we won tonight. If we'd lost, we'd have to pay double," Hans told her, sounding quite serious.

Genuine surprise showed on her face. "Really?"

"He's half-right." I shook my head and rolled my eyes at Hans. "All students with a Laney ID get everything half-price on game nights."

"Cool," Sabrina said as she handed Rhiannon her drink and sat down.

"Did you tell them you were at Mike's table?" Beth asked. I shot her a warning glance, which she characteristically ignored.

The question puzzled Sabrina. "No, why?"

"Mike's dad knows the owner really well," Rhiannon said before Beth could reply. "If they know you're here with Mike, they take good care of you." Beth looked like she was about to add something but changed her mind. I kept my mouth shut. Jill looked at me, picked up our glasses, and headed for the soda bar. I thought about stopping her but decided not to. She returned with our refills a minute or two later.

"Come on sweetie, let's dance." Jill practically pulled me to my feet. Fortunately it was a slow dance song, or the conversation we were about to have would have been rather difficult.

"Okay, Michael, explain," Jill whispered in my ear.

I figured honesty was the best policy, even if it might be kind of hard for her to believe. "I own this place. I bought the building, had it restored, and had it made into a teen club so my friends and I would have someplace to go. Hans, Beth, and Rhiannon know but not the others. The employees don't even know. They just know to run me a tab and give it to the manager. The manager deals with my dad."

Jill stopped dancing and looked me in the eye. "You're not kidding, are you?" She sounded as if she wasn't quite ready to accept the story.

My arms dropped to my sides and I shrugged. "Why would I make that up?"

After giving me a long look, she finally put her arms back around my neck and we started dancing again. "Why didn't you tell Sabrina?"

"I figured either Rhiannon would have or for some reason didn't want her to know. Those three, Hans, Beth, and Rhiannon, are on the owner's tab list even if I'm not here with them."

"Do I get to be on the list?" Jill asked coyly.

"Nope," I replied with an impish grin.

She stopped dancing and stepped back. "And why not?"

I smiled a wolfish smile. "Because you'd better not be here without me."

She smiled at that and stepped back into my arms. "I want you to ask Rhiannon to dance."

"Why?"

"So you can tell her it's okay to tell Sabrina about the list. If they're going to come here together a lot, she should know."

"Okay." We danced without talking anymore until the song was nearly over. "By the way, you are already on the list. Dad took care of it this afternoon."

"You brat," she said and kissed me.

The song ended and we returned to the table. I asked Rhiannon to dance. She looked at Jill. Jill smiled and nodded. She looked at Sabrina. Sabrina smiled and nodded. She looked back at me. I smiled and nodded. Then I laughed thinking how we must have appeared to someone watching.

Rhiannon shrugged and smiled a smile that was really more of a grimace. "What the heck. If Jill survived, maybe it won't be that bad."

I walked out onto the dance floor and Rhiannon followed. It wasn't a slow dance song, but it wasn't too fast a song either. We could talk while we danced, after a fashion.

"Considering how often we've danced, that was a mean thing to say," I said, but with a smile.

Rhiannon made an unsympathetic noise. "Yes, Michael, everyone knows what a great dancer you are." Then in a more serious tone she asked, "This was Jill's idea, wasn't it?"

"What makes you say that? Can't I ask my best friend to dance?"

"You could, but I don't think Hans will dance with you."

"You never know."

"But this was Jill's idea, right?"

"Yes, it was Jill's idea."

Momentarily satisfied with getting me to admit it, we simply danced for several measures. Then her curiosity got the better of her. "Why did Jill want you to dance with me?"

"That question, I believe, has a multipart answer. First, I think it was to show you she's not worried about us being friends from a 'Jill and Mike' as a couple perspective. Second, so I could let you know that even though I never said a word to her, she figured out you and Sabrina are a couple, and third…"

Rhiannon stopped short. "She figured out what? How did she…what made her think that?"

I said nothing.

Rhiannon nodded and began dancing again. "Okay, so she figured it out. The look you gave me after the game said you figured it out. Who else knows?"

"No one else knows as far as I know." I looked over to the table and noticed Sabrina was giving us a somewhat worried look. Figuring nothing was to be gained by saying so to Rhiannon, I thought to myself their secret wouldn't stay secret very long.

Rhiannon always could sense what I was thinking. "We would kind of like to keep it that way, you understand."

"Yeah, though that leads us to the third thing. Why didn't you tell Sabrina about the tab?"

She kind of shrugged. "I didn't want to presume."

"I'll leave it up to you to decide whether to tell her or not. For future reference, you are family to me, and family is not being presumptuous to share such things with their friends."

Rhiannon didn't respond right away, and I thought I saw a tear well up in her eye. She blinked it away and changed the subject, sort of. "Has Beth shared this with Greg?"

The idea made me cringe. "I don't know. I've never asked. I would imagine so." My dislike of Greg came across in my reply.

Rhiannon shook her head. "She hasn't, not unless you've told her it is okay to."

"I'm not sure it is okay. There's something about him I just don't like."

"Could it be the fact Beth went out with him instead of you back in seventh grade and they've been together ever since?"

"You think that may be it?" I laughed. Rhiannon always thought I was jealous of Greg. It wasn't that. He just gave me a bad feeling.

Talking to Rhiannon, I realized I was probably being silly. "You're right, I suppose. Okay, I'll tell her."

Satisfied she'd brought me around to see things her way once again, she made one more request. "Are you going to ask Beth to dance?"

"I probably won't." It didn't seem like such a good idea.

"Would you? Greg hasn't danced with her all night."

With a resigned sigh, I offered a compromise. "If there's time for another dance after the next song, I will. I'd like to dance with Jill again before closing time."

The song ended. Rhiannon took my hand, and we returned to the table. I was very aware of the feel of her hand in mine and thought I should probably pull away but couldn't bring myself to do it. With a twinge of guilt I glanced at Jill, but if it bothered her she didn't show it. From the look on Sabrina's face, it bothered her more than it did Jill. When we reached the table I realized I needed to visit the men's room and excused myself.

I'd just finished business when Greg walked in. "Sabrina's pretty hot, eh?"

Not really in the mood to talk with him, especially about the girls in our group, I gave a short answer. "She's very attractive, yes."

He gave a lecherous grin. "You think she and Rhiannon are, you know?"

Tiring quickly of his company and his comments, I replied with a curt, "I wouldn't know."

He obviously was not one to take hints. "It'd be a waste if they were, two hot chicks like them."

My temper started to rise. "Why would you care? You've got a hot chick of your own."

He shrugged. "Beth's all right, but a guy might like to try something new once in a while."

"I hope that doesn't mean what I think it means," I said, my jaw tightening. "Beth is a very good friend of mine."

Greg smirked. "Yeah, no kidding, you've been trying to get her away from me since seventh grade."

"The fact she's still with you says a lot about how she feels about you." I couldn't tell him Beth was never the girl I really wanted. I couldn't say all my talk about her dumping him for me was meant playfully. I couldn't say it to him without him using it somehow to hurt her.

A cocky grin appeared on his face. "Yeah, that's handy. What she doesn't know won't hurt her."

Suddenly all the stuff that'd happened that day unleashed itself. I grabbed Greg and threw him face first into the wall, twisted his arm up behind his back, and barely stopped myself short of pulling his shoulder right out of its socket.

"Listen to me, you sorry muscle-headed piece of trash, if you ever hurt Beth I will hunt you down and make you pay."

Beneath my grip I could feel him literally shaking in fear. "Ow. Come on Mike. It was all talk. I would never hurt Beth. Ow man. I love her, Mike. Honestly, I love her man. Ow."

I slowly relaxed and let him go. He rubbed his shoulder and straightened his shirt.

"Beth is a special girl. You had better mean what you just said. I am VERY protective of my real friends."

"Mike, man, I was just…I don't know, talking stupid. If I lost Beth, I…I just can't lose her. I've been so afraid one day she really would dump me for you." He sounded like he meant it. "Um, just for the record Mike, for my own protection, who are your real friends?"

After a couple deep breaths I had my temper under control. "Honestly, it's a short list."

Greg smiled weakly and started counting on his fingers. "Let me guess: Beth, Rhiannon, Hans..."

"And Jill," I finished for him. "If I find out you were lying to me..."

His weak smile disappeared, and genuine fear showed in his eyes. "I meant every word, Mike, I swear, and not just because I thought you were about to break me in half. Where did you learn to move like that?"

"Ancient Chinese secret." Straightening out my shirt I made sure I looked presentable. "Let's get back to our ladies, last call coming up." I had one more polite suggestion for Greg. "By the way, ask Beth to dance."

When we walked out, everyone at the table was watching us closely. What neither of us knew was that Hans had opened the door, seen what was happening, closed the door, and waited right outside. He had my back.

I don't know who was more surprised when Greg asked Beth to dance, Beth or Rhiannon. I took Jill's hand and led her to the floor. It wasn't a slow dance, but I pulled her close and held her tight anyway.

"What happened between you and Greg in the Men's Room," she asked almost as though she wasn't sure she wanted to know.

"We had a spiritual meeting of the minds, and I read him the book of Don't-Mess-With-Mike's-Friends."

Jill looked confused but wisely decided not to pursue the point. "Some time I'll ask you to explain exactly what that means."

As she laid her head on my shoulder, I looked over at Beth and Greg. Beth looked at me and beamed a huge smile. We turned slowly to the music, and I noticed Wes and Allie were on the dance floor, too. Finally I looked back towards the table and there sat Sabrina and Rhiannon smiling at us and holding hands under the table. It had been a heck of a day.

Fourteen

November, 1976

Since my birthday fell on Veterans' Day and the Drivers' License office was closed, I had to wait until the day after I turned sixteen to get my driver's license. I took the road test in my mother's Buick LeSabre. That was my dad's idea. He didn't think showing up in my GTO would make a very good impression on the examiner. I only missed one question on the written test and did well on the road test, so the State of North Carolina granted me a driver's license.

As soon as we got home I jumped in my car, a restored 1966 Pontiac GTO convertible, and drove to Jill's house to show her my driver's license. My best friend Hans was very understanding when I told him Jill would be my first passenger; after all, he had a Y chromosome too.

Jill and I had been together as a couple since the first Friday night football game. Her folks were fond of me, and my mom and dad adored Jill. The four adults talked it over and agreed that as a reward for getting my license, Jill and I could go on our first car date.

The sun had just dropped below the tree tops when I pulled my GTO into Jill's driveway. Practically leaping from the car, I hustled to her porch and rang the bell. Jill answered the door. Glancing at the driveway, she saw the GTO and knew what it meant. "All right, let's see your driver's license."

With what I'm sure was the dumbest grin in history plastered to my face, I handed over my newly minted driver's license. "Not a bad picture; it almost looks like you. Hey, Mom, Mike's here. Guess what? He got his license."

Cierra congratulated me on achieving that milestone. After a gentle reminder from Jill, she gave me a polite admonishment to drive carefully taking her daughter on our first car date. "I'll tell your father when he gets home, dear. I'm sure he'll be thrilled with the news."

Jill raised her eyebrows and gave her mother a doubtful look. "Oh, I can just imagine."

"I'll be very careful, Cierra."

Jill gave her mom a quick hug before walking with me to the car. I gallantly opened the door for her, went around to the driver's side, cranked the engine, and backed out of the drive on my first car date. I took her to the Linguini Grill as I knew it was her favorite restaurant. They didn't actually grill linguini, but the food was pretty good. The hostess on duty, Kate, beamed when she saw me walk in with Jill. Kate and my mom were in a ladies' club together. "I guess this means somebody's gotten his driver's license."

Before I could reply, Jill announced, "Yes, he did. And like the good boyfriend he is, the first place he drove was to pick me up for our first un-chaperoned date."

Kate smiled at her before giving me a knowing look. "Well then, since this is your first real date we must make it special." I knew that look meant we weren't quite as un-chaperoned as Jill might've thought.

Kate escorted us to a somewhat secluded table. Once we were seated, she assured us our waitress would be along shortly and made her way to the bar. The bartender soon appeared with a wine bucket full of ice. "Sir, ma'am, your sparkling beverage."

He turned our wine glasses up and pulled a bottle of sparkling white grape juice from the ice. He made a great show of opening the bottle and pouring just a bit into my glass. Not sure what to do, I picked up the glass and tasted the juice.

"Does the gentleman find the choice to his liking?"

Trying to sound like I knew what I was doing, I replied, "Oh yes, it's very nice, thank you." He smiled and filled our glasses. After replacing the bottle in the ice, he returned to the bar.

Jill seemed quite impressed. "Wow! That was so cool. They've never done that when I've come in with my folks."

Our waitress arrived with menus. She told us her name was Leigh and invited us to take a few minutes to think about what we would like. Jill and I began looking over the menu.

Jill lowered her menu and looked across the table. "I always get the spaghetti plate, but that doesn't seem right for tonight. It's more like a kid's meal. I don't feel like a kid tonight."

I looked at her and thought to myself she didn't look like a kid either. She looked beautiful. Clearly she hadn't doubted I'd get my license and show up for our date. "The manicotti is very good, especially if you like ricotta and mozzarella cheese. If you want something special, try the veal parmesan. It's my favorite."

She looked the menu over once more before sitting back and folding her hands on the table. "Okay, Mike, I'll trust you on this one. I'll try the veal. What're you gonna have?"

There were so many delicious items on the menu, I was stuck picking one. "I can't decide between the stuffed shells and the veal." While I was trying to decide, inspiration hit. "Since you're having the veal, I'll get the stuffed shells. Then you can try some of mine and I can sample some of yours."

"Sounds like a great idea."

Between the salad, the breadsticks, and the meal, neither of us had room for dessert. The food was excellent, and the staff went out of their way to make us feel special. I showed my appreciation with a generous tip.

It was a school night, and I'd promised to have Jill home by ten. That didn't leave us much time after dinner for a movie or anything, so we settled for a drive to the beach. Slipping out of our shoes, we walked across the dunes to watch the waves breaking in the moonlight.

Waves lapped gently at the shore as we stood, arms around each other, admiring the view. "Mike, this has been a great first date."

"I'm glad you enjoyed it, though technically it wasn't our first date."

She snuggled closer to me. "I know, but it kind of was. It was the first time we went out without someone's parents driving and some of our friends along."

"It's been nice just being the two of us, hasn't it?"

Jill sighed a contented sigh. "Yes, very nice."

Moon light reflected on the waves, and the only sound was the sound of the surf. Jill turned towards me, and I pulled her close. Brushing back her hair, I slowly lowered my lips to hers. It wasn't a quick high school crush kiss; it was a real 'I want you' kiss. Jill responded in kind. If we'd had more time, who knows where that kiss might've led? I felt so close to Jill. I was so glad she was in my life. I wanted so much to be in love with her. I really did.

She pulled away and looked me in the eye. "Mike, right now most couples would profess some kind of undying love for each other. Let's not. I like you. I like you a lot. I like being with you. But let's not say love."

Was she reading my mind? "Jill, if you like me, that's enough for me." What a safe, cowardly answer. Apparently it was enough. She pulled my head down for another lingering kiss. Then we had to go.

Fifteen

Jill and I were deep in like and mutual desire. We spent every moment together we could until Christmas Break. Then came our first real test. Jill was going to Asheville to spend time with her grandmother. Hans and I were booked for Europe to visit his. We'd be on separate continents for ten long days.

The day before Hans and I left for Spain, I took Jill to dinner at the Bridge Tender, a locally famous seafood restaurant on the waterway right by the drawbridge. After dinner I set a wrapped present on the table. So she wouldn't forget me while we were apart, I gave Jill a golden heart locket for Christmas. Draping it carefully around her neck, I opened the clasp to show her the picture inside. It was one taken in the little photo booth at Lumina Pier.

"It's beautiful, Michael. I love it." I half expected her to say she loved me, but instead she hugged me and gave me a kiss. "You'll have to wait until you drop me off to get your present."

My present was a charcoal drawing Jill made of me at the helm of Hey 19. "I drew it from that picture I took of you the first time you took me sailing."

I knew Jill liked to draw, but she'd always been shy about showing me her work. Looking at that picture, I couldn't understand why. "This is awesome, Jill. You're really good."

A humble smile curled her lips. "My dad made the frame. It's oak. Ellis likes to mess around with wood."

"If this frame is him messing around, he must create some masterpieces when he tries."

Reluctant to say good-bye, we lingered in the living room until Cierra politely asked what time my flight was the next day. Taking her subtle hint, Jill walked me to the door for one more goodnight kiss. Holding her close, I whispered "Merry Christmas, sweetheart." Jill's arms tightened around me. "Merry Christmas, Mike, I'm gonna miss you." One more quick kiss, then home.

January eventually arrived, and our long separation ended. Soon after school started, it was time for the NJROTC Ball, a formal event where the male cadets wore dress blues while their dates and the female cadets dressed up in evening gowns. By happy coincidence the Ball took place on Jill's birthday.

The evening of the Ball I showed up at Jill's house with several surprises. She was expecting me to pick her up in my GTO and stared in disbelief when she saw my ride. "Michael, what in the world, a limousine?"

"Of course it's a limousine. Only the best for my lady on her birthday," I said as if ordering up a limo was something I did on a regular basis.

Cierra rested her hand on Jill's shoulder in a reassuring gesture. "Michael, I think it's quite nice."

Ellis said simply, "I'm impressed."

Taking Jill's hand, I led her to the limo. The chauffeur bowed to Jill before opening the back door and helping her in. In the limo another surprise awaited Jill. The interior was decorated with Sweet Sixteen banners and balloons. Not only that, I'd talked her mom into convincing Jill not to wear any jewelry with the dress. Now she'd find out why.

"I got you a little something for your birthday," I said handing her a slender package.

"Michael, what have you done?" Jill asked with a smile that told me she had some idea. As she opened the box her breath caught and tears welled in her eyes. "Oh, Michael, they're beautiful," she said, taking the string of pearls from the box. "Oh, put them on me, Michael. They're perfect."

I fastened the pearls around her neck. There was a small mirror in the limo and she admired herself for a moment. The white pearls shimmered against her black gown as if lit from within.

"Michael, they're so beautiful, thank you," Jill said as she grabbed me and kissed me.

Gently pulling free, I said, "You're not quite finished. Check the box."

Looking into the box, she found the matching pearl earrings. "Oh, my goodness, Michael, this is too much."

"They're a matched set." Jill rolled her eyes at my innocent expression. Using the mirror, she put the earrings on. The effect of the necklace and earrings with her black dress was stunning. The second kiss they earned me was equally stunning. "Happy Birthday, baby," I said when I caught my breath.

"Oh thank you, Michael, thank you, thank you, thank you."

We arrived at the hall where the ball was taking place. The maitre'd checked our pass before signaling a waiter to escort us to our table.

Jill was impressed. "They've really gone all out on this, haven't they?"

Looking around at how grandly the hall was done up, I decided telling Jill about the rather sizeable donation made so they could go all out wasn't really necessary. Simply agreeing with her seemed like a better idea. "You're right, the place looks great."

Wesley was already there with Alyssa but seated at a different table. I noticed several people, mostly the guys, noticing Jill, and stood a little straighter. Jill noticed and smiled at me.

Dinner was good, if somewhat ordinary. We had a choice between beef tips au juice with baked potato and vegetable medley or roast chicken breast on rice with peas. I opted for the beef tips. Jill had the chicken. We ate, announcements were made, awards were given, and then we danced.

Around midnight the announcement was made for the last dance. It was a song by Fleetwood Mac. It was "Rhiannon." A twinge perhaps? No, I think not. Jill, with a touch of green in those amber eyes, looked at me. I smiled and reached out to take her hand. "Let's dance, my beautiful birthday girl."

"Let's dance, Mike," Jill replied as she stood and moved into my arms.

And we danced.

Sixteen

There's no more important holiday for high school sweethearts than Valentine's Day. I spent the time between Jill's birthday and Valentine's Day trying to come up with some wonderful way to celebrate it with her. Growing desperate for ideas, I turned to my two best sources, Beth and Rhiannon. They were at Rhiannon's house preparing decorations for the Valentine's Dance. "I need your help. I can't decide what to give Jill for Valentine's Day."

Beth had a ready answer. "Flowers are always nice. Greg always gives me roses. He adds one for each Valentine's we've been together."

Rhiannon's face softened and she smiled. "Aw, that's sweet. I don't know why, but Greg seems more mellow lately."

Beth nodded thoughtfully. "Ever since he and Michael had their talk, he's been like a whole new boyfriend."

Rhiannon tilted her head and gave me a suspicious look. "Really? Michael, what did you say to him?"

I was surprised she didn't already know. "I told him if he didn't start treating Beth the way she deserved to be treated, I'd break his arm."

Rhiannon's expression showed she was not amused. "You are a funny guy - oh wait, that's not funny. What did you really tell him?"

Beth intervened on my behalf. "Rhiannon, that is about what Mike told him. Greg told me himself when I asked what brought about such a pleasant change."

"Michael, I'm surprised at you." Rhiannon clearly didn't approve of my strong-arm tactics.

Obviously neither of them knew the whole story. I couldn't really blame Greg for not telling Beth exactly why I'd gone off on him. "Yeah, well, I was kind of having a bad day."

"Was that the day…" Rhiannon asked, and paused. She looked stricken as she remembered what else happened that day.

With an irritated smirk, I nodded and confirmed that was the day.

"Oh," Rhiannon said.

Beth sat quietly through our exchange, but her eyes were darting back and forth between Rhiannon and me. After several seconds of awkward silence, she suggested it would be best if we got back to the subject at hand. "What should Mike get Jill for Valentine's? I think a nice bouquet of red roses would be perfect."

I rubbed my chin. "Don't red roses signify love?"

"Well, yes," Beth said. Then she smiled shyly. "Greg always gives me red roses."

I let out a resigned sigh and shook my head. "Then red roses wouldn't be appropriate. Jill and I aren't in love."

Rhiannon dropped the scissors she was using to cut out little construction paper hearts. "What do you mean?" she asked sharply. "You love her, don't you?"

Startled by her reaction, I tried to explain. "I like Jill a lot, a whole lot. I like being with her, making her happy, going out with her, but I don't love her." Even as I said it I felt an empty space inside where that love should have been. Biting my lip, I looked at Rhiannon and knew why Jill couldn't fill it.

Beth tilted her head and gave me a hard look. She hadn't missed the way my eyes fell on Rhiannon. "And Jill knows all this?"

Rhiannon returned my gaze, but if she knew what I was thinking, gave no sign. Beth was waiting for an answer. "As far as I know she does. She told me that's how she feels about me."

Rhiannon stood up and took a few steps toward the window. "You've got to be kidding me. Everyone at school thinks you two are the most in-love couple since Romeo and Juliet, when in fact you aren't in love at all." Rhiannon sounded slightly puzzled and yet something else tinged her voice, too.

I took a step toward her, almost daring her to back away. "I don't know. Maybe we are in love and just won't admit it to each other," I said, looking her hard in the eye.

She made a dismissive snort and pushed past me. "Bro, you are certifiably insane. You and Jill both are. Of all the people you know, only the two of you don't know you're in love." Rhiannon sat down and resumed cutting up the construction paper. I noticed that instead of little hearts she was just making random cuts.

"Rhiannon, go easy on him," Beth interjected. "Jill and I have talked about this."

We both turned to stare at Beth. "You have?" I asked.

"She says what Mike says with one small difference." She reached out and put her hand on my arm. "Mike, Jill thinks you do love her."

My eyes twitched back and forth. For a second I couldn't focus. "She does?"

Rhiannon put the paper and scissors down. "Suddenly you're a man of very few words."

I blinked my eyes rapidly several times trying to regain my focus. "I am," I stammered. The tension broke like glass under a hammer and we all started laughing.

"Whether they're in love or head over heels in like," Beth said, "Mike still has to pick a Valentine's Day present." But we never settled on anything.

It was my Dad who finally found my solution for me. "Mike, I have a wild idea for you. Why don't you name a star after Jillian?"

Naturally I was somewhat skeptical. "What a great idea, Dad. How in the world would I go about doing it?"

Holding up a brochure he'd received in the mail, Dad said, "I've got the names right here of some folks up in Illinois who want to start up what they're calling the International Star Registry."

It was an intriguing idea. "That's so weird it might actually work. Tell me more."

"Well, according to their literature the star's name would be filed with the Library of Congress. You get a star chart showing where in the night sky it is and a certificate from the registry. You can also get a sterling silver, star-shaped medallion engraved with the name of the star and its celestial coordinates."

A star would definitely be a unique Valentine's Day present. "If they can get it all done and to me in time for Valentine's Day, let's do it."

Dad contacted them, and they named a star after Jill. It was one of the first they'd done. They sent a nice packet including all they promised, and it arrived in time.

As Valentine's Day approached Jill let me know she had something special planned for the occasion. "Since Valentine's is on a Monday, I thought we could celebrate Sunday night instead," she said. "You can come over to the house, and I will cook you a nice dinner. We can have a romantic evening alone."

A romantic evening alone sounded great, but I wondered how she'd manage it. "What about your folks?"

With a coy smile Jill replied, "They're going to Asheville Friday and won't be back until Tuesday."

"They're letting you stay home alone over the weekend, over Valentine's Day?"

Her smile widened as she slowly nodded yes. "Not only that, me inviting you over and cooking you dinner was their idea." Then she winced a little. "They said they felt like they could trust us. I promised them they could."

When I told my parents what Jill had planned for Valentine's Day, I expected them to the kill the idea. Boy, was I surprised.

"It sounds like a wonderful evening. How sweet of Jill to think to do something like that," Mom said. What neither Jill nor I knew then was that Ellis and Cierra talked to my mom and dad before deciding it would be okay.

Dad took me into his study. "Mike, I know I can trust you, but I also know what it's like to be a teenage boy on the verge of manhood." I really hated it when he talked like that. "What I'm saying is, should anything happen, not that it should, just be careful. Do you know what I mean?" Dad put his hand on my shoulder and looked me in the eye.

"I understand, Dad, thanks." I understood exactly what he meant; nothing better happen.

He smiled and patted me on the back. "That's what Dads are for, Mike."

When the evening for the dinner came, I put the Star Registry stuff into the GTO along with a mixed bouquet of light pink and coral roses. The florist told me light pink indicated fun and happiness, and the coral colored ones denoted desire. I felt that expressed things nicely.

Since it was going to be such a special occasion, I dressed up a bit for the dinner - shirt and tie, slacks, a nice leather jacket.

I was glad I did when Jill answered the door in a beautiful pink mid-length dress and heels. "Hi, Mike, Happy Valentine's," she said almost shyly.

"Happy Valentine's, sweetheart." I kissed her lightly on the lips while handing her the roses. "These are for you."

Holding them close so she could enjoy their fragrance, she smiled. "They're beautiful, Michael. Do you know what the colors mean?"

The way she asked I knew she did. "The florist told me. I hope you like them."

"I think they're beautiful." She gestured toward the other items I was carrying. "What else have you got there?"

Turning slightly as if trying to hide them, I said, "If I can come inside, I'll show you."

Jill laughed as she realized we were still standing on the porch and practically dragged me into the house. She led me to the living room where we sat down on the sofa.

"OK, now you're in. May I please see what else you've brought?" she asked with exaggerated politeness. I'd wrapped it all together with the pendant in a box on top. The certificate was under that and the star chart on the bottom. Jill looked puzzled as she finished opening the packages. "It's a beautiful pendant, Mike, but what does all this mean?"

Triumphantly I announced, "Baby, I had a star named after you."

Jill sat stunned for a moment. "Can you do that? I mean, how'd ya do that? A star, I have a star named after me?"

Not sure if she was pleased or disappointed, I quickly explained. "Yes, a star, at those coordinates there. If we're lucky it's clear enough tonight for us to see it. Bring the star chart." I got up, took her hand, and led her to the backyard. Then we went back inside to find a flashlight. On the way out we turned out all the lights. Using the flashlight to read the star chart, it only took a few minutes to find her star. Silently I thanked my sailing instructor for those lessons on celestial navigation.

My arm around her shoulder, I was pointing toward the heavens. "See the big bright star? It's really a planet. Now drop your gaze down about a foot and then to the right about six inches. See that star right there? That's Jillian Jonas. Sweetheart, that's your star."

Jill swallowed hard. With a bit of a catch in her voice she said, "You bought me a star. What kind of guy buys his girl a star for Valentine's?" Oh, no, I began to think, this was a really bad idea. "Only the greatest boyfriend in the world would. That's you Michael Lanier. A star, my star, it's right up there. Wow." Maybe it wasn't such a bad idea after all.

I felt Jill shiver and suggested we go back inside. Before we did she turned in my arms, pulled my head down towards hers, and kissed me. She looked so happy. "I wish…" she began softly, then stopped. "Never mind. Come on." She took my hand and led me toward the house. "Dinner is keeping warm in the oven. I hope you like it. I've never made it before, but I remembered from our first "real" date you mentioning you like manicotti. So I found a recipe and tried to make it. I hope you like it."

A delicious aroma filled the kitchen when she opened the oven. "It smells wonderful. I'm sure I'll love it."

Jill tossed a salad, and we started with that. She also made some bread, light on the garlic. "You do know why I went light on the garlic, don't you?" she asked with a sly smile.

"I hope the reason you did is the same reason I'm glad you did."

The salad done, I took the manicotti out of the oven while Jill got down the plates. Suddenly I was struck with a feeling of how nice this felt. "Jill, doesn't this feel…I don't know…but I like it."

Setting the plates down, she said, without turning around, "I know; I like it too. It's almost like we're, well, let's eat." Neither of us seemed able to put it into words.

The manicotti was wonderful. I tried not to eat too much. It was hard because I wanted to eat a lot more. After dinner we cleaned up and returned to the couch. Jill wanted to know more about her gift. "Tell me more about my star. How did you do it?"

I explained to her how I'd been trying to find something special for Valentine's Day and how my Dad came across a brochure from the Registry people.

With a smug look Jill said, "I knew you asked for help finding something."

"You did, how?"

"Girls talk, you know," Jill said with a cute little laugh. Laughing along with her, I noted I would have to keep that in mind. "Anyway, I think it is the best Valentine's present ever."

Her demeanor changed slightly; I don't know quite how to describe the difference. She reached up and brushed the backs of her fingers along my cheek. A tingle went down my spine. Jill put her arms around my neck and pulled me close. I leaned toward her and our lips met. The kiss became more intense and passionate. Before it could go too far, we pulled back.

I took a deep breath and let it out slowly. I couldn't help but think that had things been just a little different for us, we could be in love. I thought it would be nice to be in love with Jill, but you can't make your heart behave as your mind says it should.

"It'll be time for you to head home soon," Jill reluctantly observed.

"I wish I could stay here with you tonight. I'm really going to hate to leave."

"I love hearing you say that," Jill said, pulling me towards her once more. It was as close as she ever came to saying she loved me. All too soon it was time for me to go.

Standing on the porch we held each other, reluctant to let the evening end. "Mike, naming a star for me is the sweetest thing you could possibly have done. Years from now when we've gone our separate ways, I'll be able to look up at Star Jillian Jonas and think of that wonderful guy I knew in high school who thought I was special enough to name a star for."

Her calm acceptance of our eventual parting should have stung, but it didn't. Inside I knew, just as she did, it was inevitable. Still, I wasn't ready to give up on us just yet. "Don't start missing me yet, Jill. We've still got high school to get through, and who knows? Maybe there's a chance it won't end with graduation."

My insisting we had a chance brought a sad yet hopeful smile to her face. "You're right Mike. Graduation is more than two long years away. There's always hope. And that's two long years of fun we can have to make memories."

"Happy Valentine's, Jill," I said and I kissed her good-night.

"Happy Valentine's, Mike, see you tomorrow." She kissed me one more time.

I walked to my car without looking back until I rounded the hood and reached my door. Jill stood there watching me leave. I knew I'd see her the next day, yet somehow I felt like I'd lost something. She smiled and waved and then went into the house. As the door closed behind her, I climbed into the car and headed for home. It occurred to me as I drove along that what I'd lost was an opportunity.

Seventeen

Jill and I made the most of our time after Valentine's Day. As winter gave way to spring, I taught her to sail. She took flying lessons with me. She came to Camp and spent three weeks during the summer after sophomore year. In the fall she took scuba lessons. We did everything we could to bring us closer.

We even took ballroom dancing lessons. Our friends laughed at us until the homecoming dance, and then they all wanted to know where we learned those moves. Jill came to every soccer game. We went to every football and basketball game together. I went to all her chorale recitals. We spent every moment we could together and tried our best to fall in love. We liked and enjoyed one another but just couldn't find that together forever we wanted so badly. By the end of junior year we knew it wasn't going to happen. We decided to take the summer completely off from each other and see how things seemed come senior year. Jill headed off to Asheville, and I headed to Camp.

In addition to my work at camp, there was my River Dream project. After my first summer at Camp, I knew I wanted a place of my own on the river. I told my dad. At his suggestion my trust fund acquired a significant piece of land along the river next to Camp. The property boasted an old fishing cottage, a rickety dock, and a grass airstrip once used by crop dusters. The fishing cottage is where I stayed while working at camp. We'd made some improvements to the dock, including adding a screened room at the shore end. The summer before senior year, ground was broken for a house to replace the cottage.

Junior year ended on June ninth. Jill left for Asheville June tenth. I flew my restored Piper Cub to River Dream on Sunday morning, June eleventh. Those of us on staff had one week to get everything ready before summer's first campers arrived. There were cabins to be cleaned, shower houses to be sanitized, a dining hall to prepare, and most important to me, sailboats to be rigged.

Chase Arnold, one of the other counselors and a good friend, arrived just after lunch. Just under six feet tall with a lean build and brown hair he kept cut short, he'd always been popular with most of the girls at Camp. Chase was something of a sailing phenomenon. He could read the wind like no one I ever knew. For the rest of us, racing against him in our weekly regattas was usually a contest to see who'd finish second.

The next counselor to arrive was Maeve Dalton, a girl who'd been in the Counselor Training program the year before. Back then she was all knees and elbows. What a difference a year can make. When she stepped out of the car in her white tank top and cut-off jeans, Chase and I practically tripped over each other to be the first to greet her. Chase outmaneuvered me and got there first.

"Hi, you're Maeve, right? I'm Chase."

"Yes, I remember you, Chase," Maeve said without much enthusiasm. Then with a careless toss of her strawberry blond hair she turned her heather blue eyes on me and smiled. "Hi, Mike."

The way she smiled gave me a warm feeling inside. "Hi, Maeve, nice to see you again." I tried not to notice the disappointment on Chase's face.

Her father - I recognized him from the previous summer - pulled her bags out of the trunk and set them on the ground next to her. "Will you need some help with those, Maeve?" With a slight nod toward me and Chase, he seemed to indicate it looked like she probably had plenty of willing assistance.

She turned to him and said, "No, Dad. You don't have to hang around." He hugged her quickly and wished her a good summer. As he drove off Maeve turned her dazzling smile on me again. "I'm glad you're here this year, Mike. I was hoping you would be."

"Really," I said, somewhat surprised.

"Yeah. You were so helpful to us CT's last year," Maeve said, referring to the counselor trainees. "I was nervous about working this summer, but with you here, I know I'll be fine."

Naturally I was flattered. "Thanks for the vote of confidence."

Chase was nothing if not persistent. "Maeve, I can help you carry your gear to your cabin."

Not interested in his help but not wanting to hurt his feelings, Maeve politely declined. "That's okay. I think Mike and I can handle it."

The expression on Chase's face was priceless. I just looked at him and shrugged. He shook his head with a crooked smile. "Then I guess I'll see you around. Let me know if you need anything."

"Thanks Chase, I will," she said. Picking up one of her bags, she waited expectantly. Resigning myself to the not-so-arduous task of helping her, I picked up her two bigger bags and let her lead me toward the office where she would check in and get her cabin assignment.

Maeve was assigned as a Schooner Counselor. Schooners were kids eleven to fifteen years old who stayed at camp two straight weeks, from Sunday afternoon until two Saturdays later. Since I was on sailing staff, I got see a lot of her as a Schooner's time at camp was spent mostly on the water, when they weren't in it swimming.

Friday evening near the end of Maeve's first two-week stint found us sitting on the dock fishing with the campers. In deference to the hot, humid air we were wearing the unofficial summer uniforms of Camp Riversail. Chase and I had on our Birdwell Beach Britches. They were comfortable, dried quickly, and made perfect summer sailing shorts. Maeve, like most girls at Camp, wore a bikini, a pale yellow one with paler blue polka-dots.

We all fished with cane poles. Our bait was squid. Thanks to the brackish waters near Camp, we usually caught salt water species like croaker and pin fish. Chase, Maeve, and I put our poles aside and chatted while keeping an eye on the kids.

"I just don't know what to do on my time off," Maeve said. "I can't really go anywhere, but I don't want to just stay here on camp."

Sensing an opening, Chase suggested, "Maybe you and I could go to New Bern for a movie or something."

His idea didn't seem to interest her. "I don't know. Mike, what're you doing?"

I glanced helplessly at Chase before replying. He shrugged and gestured his surrender. Maeve either didn't notice, or pretended not to.

"Actually I'm taking delivery of a new sailboat," I said giving Chase a sideways look.

Curiosity gleamed in her eyes. "Really, what kind?"

Seeing her interest was genuine, I told her a little about it. "She's a nineteen-foot Mariner. They're built at a boat yard up in Maine. She's about the size of a Scott but has a small cabin. The builder is sending a representative down with the boat to make sure it's ship shape and ready to go when I pick it up. She'll have an all-blue hull with a red stripe at the waterline." Feeling I was getting a bit carried away, I stopped.

"It sounds really nice," Maeve said appreciatively. Then she waited expectantly.

Starting to get a sense she might like to come along, I told her, "Chase was going to help me sail her down from Oriental." I wasn't sure she'd want to go if she knew he'd be along. They got along well enough on the job, but spending her day off with him on a boat might not be her idea of fun.

Chase bristled when I said "was." "I still am."

How he reconciled that to having just asked Maeve to the movies at a time we'd be out on the river was a mystery to me. "Chase is going to help me sail her down from Oriental," I modified, "would you like to come?"

Looking at Chase as if deciding whether she could put up with him on the short voyage from Oriental back to Camp, she finally shrugged. Reaching out and resting her hand lightly on my arm, she looked into my eyes and said, "I'd love to."

My arm felt very warm under her hand. Suddenly I was slightly nervous. "Great, we'll leave Saturday just before lunch. That way we can grab a bite in Oriental and then head to the Marina."

A potential glitch in the plan occurred to Maeve. "How are we going to get there?"

"Captain Jack said he'll take us," I explained. Captain Jack was the Camp Sailing Master.

Saturday morning Chase took me aside to inform me he was going to have to beg off on picking up the boat. "Liana asked me if I'd take her to New Bern to the mall. I suggested maybe we take in a movie and she said sure."

"Chase, man, I can't believe you're abandoning me. I don't like the idea of sailing a new boat down solo."

"You won't be solo. You'll have the lovely Maeve for a crew," Chase winked. "The way I see it I'm doing you a favor."

"Oh really, just how do you figure?"

He was ready for that question. Sitting there on his bunk, he ticked the reasons off on his fingers. "Well, in the first place she's a pretty decent sailor. In the second place she's pretty decent looking. In the third place she digs you. I'm giving you a chance to spend a few hours at sea with one of the best-looking staff members on camp." He spread his hands and grinned triumphantly.

Realizing I wasn't going to change his mind, I plopped down on my bunk. "Chase, I don't need that kind of chance. I'm trying to get over a girl, not find a new one."

His expression was that of a frustrated teacher talking to a difficult pupil. "Mike, you'll do alright. Maeve is a good sailor. I trained her myself. You've sailed with her, you know she is. Think what this'll do for her confidence." Leaning close across the space between our bunks, he confided, "Besides, I couldn't even get to the plate with Maeve. Liana is at least giving me a chance at bat."

I had to laugh. "Baseball analogies, Chase, you must be hard up. Okay, you've made your point. Maeve's a competent sailor. Go enjoy your date with Liana."

Maeve didn't seem too disappointed to learn Chase abandoned us. In fact, she seemed downright pleased. That made me a little uncomfortable, but I told myself to wise up and enjoy the prospect of spending the afternoon on the river with this good looking lady. Just before noon we signed out at the Camp office and loaded ourselves into Captain Jack's Jeep Cherokee. First we swung by the cottage to pick up some gear I thought we'd need. Then we piled back into the Cherokee.

Maeve leaned forward from the back seat. "That's a nice little cottage, Mike. Is it your folks' place?"

I turned around in my seat as far as the seat belt would let me. "No, it's mine," I told her honestly.

She looked surprised but took me at my word. "All yours, cool. Do you know who's building the house across the street?"

Captain Jack might have started to say something but instead just kind of snorted. I gave him a sharp look. "It's mine, too. I mean, I'm having it built. When it's done I'll move in."

That was too much for her. Owning a cottage at my age, okay, possible, building myself a house, no way. "Now I know you're putting me on."

Captain Jack glanced at her in the rear view mirror. "No, Maeve, there's more to our Michael here than meets the eye."

By then I was feeling decidedly uncomfortable. "Maeve, it's like this. I inherited a little money from my godfather and invested it in some land here on the river, and in that house. Some of it I used to buy the sailboat we're picking up today. It's no big deal really." Captain Jack looked at me as if to say, good story, boy, stick to it.

Maeve sat back and rested her chin on her hand. "Oh, I see now. I inherited some money from my grandma. Daddy put it in the bank to help pay for my college. I'm applying to Brown and Yale. He says the inheritance will just about cover it, and he wishes I'd go to State or UNC."

"Brown and Yale are good schools." I thought to myself that they were good schools if you were into the whole Ivy League thing.

"I keep getting letters from 'em about how interested they are in me going there. My guidance counselor says it's unusual for a rising junior to get such interest from top schools like those." Maybe there was more to her than I realized. "Sometimes I wish my parents had let them put me up a grade when my second grade teacher recommended it. I'd be a senior now."

We arrived at Scoops, a nice little restaurant and dairy bar in Oriental. I treated for lunch before we headed to the Marina. The Marina was both an actual marina and also the swankiest hotel and restaurant in Oriental. The boatyard representative was waiting for us at the Marina when we got there. Dad saw to all the paperwork ahead of time, so all I needed was some familiarization with the new boat and I'd be ready to go. Jack hung around until he was sure I was ready to sail, just in case.

The boat - I hadn't picked a name for her yet - was already in the water. We went aboard, and the rep went over everything with us. Then he started the motor and took us out onto the river where he made sure we knew how to rig the boat for sail, trim the sheets, control the helm, and all those little basics you need to familiarize yourself with when you get a new boat. Finally he declared us ready to go, and we returned to the Marina. "You seem to know what you're doing, Mr. Lanier. I feel confident you'll enjoy your Mariner."

I looked the boat over from stem to stern, running through my head everything he'd gone over until satisfied I had no more questions. "Thank you sir, I'm sure I will."

He left us to head for Raleigh and begin his trek back to Maine. Jack asked if we were ready to set sail because, if so, he needed to get going himself. After assuring him we were, he watched us motor out onto the river before he left.

Once clear of the harbor we hoisted sail, trimmed the sheets, and set course for River Dream. I plotted a course back and forth across the river that gave us plenty of opportunity to practice tacking at several different points of sail. We set off on a starboard tack on a beam reach. Maeve worked the jib sheet while I manned the main sheet and the helm. The boat responded beautifully. She was the same length over all as Hey 19 but had a different look and feel about her.

I'd been concentrating on the boat, but when it was time to make the first tack I suddenly noticed Maeve. She was sitting up on the starboard rail, looking forward, with her strawberry blond hair blowing back in the wind. Her long tan legs were spread just so as she balanced herself. Though she had cleated the jib sheet, she still kept the bitter end loosely in her hand. Her head moved back and forth, up and down, as she first scanned the water ahead and then the jib checking to be sure we had clear sailing and good trim. Forcing my attention back to the task at hand, I called out, "Prepare to tack."

"Ready," she answered as she quickly firmed her grip on the jib sheet and loosed it from the cleat. I pushed the rudder over and as the bow came through the wind ducked under the boom, passed the tiller and main sheet from one hand to the other, straightened up the tiller as the sails caught wind, trimmed up the main sheet, and finally looked to check on Maeve with the jib sheet. There she sat on the port rail, jib trimmed smartly, back into her rhythm of checking the waters ahead and the jib above.

I was very impressed. Chase'd been right about her. She was not only an attractive lady, she made a fine crew. "Maeve, would you like to take the tiller?"

"Are you serious? Yes, I'd love to." She checked to see the jib sheet was secure on the cleat and cautiously made her way to the stern. I told her what to watch for with the helm and main sheet, then made my way forward to stand by on the jib sheet. Now it was my turn to keep one eye out on the river and one on the jib. I added one thing to this routine. Now and again I would let my gaze linger on Maeve at the helm. She looked so natural. She just seemed to love it. When it was time for the next tack I asked her if she wanted to take it.

Her expression told me she thought that was a silly question. "If you think you can handle the jib sheet," she replied. Chuckling at her reaction, I assured her I thought I could manage.

"Prepare to tack," she ordered. I no sooner said "Ready" than she pushed over the tiller and we were swinging across the wind. I may have been a half a heart beat late on the jib, but if she noticed she didn't say anything.

We took turns at the helm the rest of the afternoon and near sundown finally headed to the dock at River Dream. As I hadn't had any experience bringing a boat into the dock at River Dream, under sail or otherwise, I decided to drop sail and motor up to the dock.

"What's the matter, Mike, chicken?" Maeve teased.

Leaning out over the starboard rail to check our approach, I countered that I was being prudently cautious. "This is the first time I've brought a boat into this dock."

Maeve was enough of a sailor to understand. "Then better to be cautious." She giggled. "Did you really just use 'prudently' in a sentence?"

"Why, yes, I believe I did." As we closed the remaining distance I called out, "Prepare to dock."

"Aye, aye, sir," Maeve quipped as she leaped nimbly to the dock to secure the bowline.

I surveyed the boat lift, trying to figure out just how I was going to get the boat into it. When it was installed the contractor went over the controls with me, but I hadn't actually lifted a boat with it.

As I puzzled over the controls, Maeve gave me a dubious stare. "You've never done this before either?"

"Everybody does something for first time once."

She smiled and then laughed. "That sounds like a Chinese proverb."

"How hard can it be?" I asked.

It was harder than I thought, but through perseverance and thanks to Maeve insisting I read the directions on the lift, we got the job done without too much foul language on my part.

Once I was sure the boat was secure in its cradle, we headed up to the cottage. "It's time for a nice cold drink, and then I'll take you back to camp."

"I wonder if I'll be in time for supper," Maeve said absently.

Checking my watch I realized she probably wouldn't be. "Supper's not a problem. Since you were such an adequate crew member, I shall cook you dinner."

She bristled at being described as adequate before realizing I just said it to get under her skin. In retaliation she scoffed, "You, cook me dinner. This ought to be good."

"I beg your pardon. I happen to be a very good cook."

With a doubtful laugh she looked at me over the top of her sunglasses. "I'll be the judge of that."

Suddenly it was very important to me that she didn't hurry off back to Camp. "So you'll stay for dinner?"

"It's a date," she said with a smile and a twinkle in her beautiful blue eyes.

As I opened the cottage door to let her in, my thoughts interestingly enough weren't about Jill. Rather, I wondered what Rhiannon would think of me cooking dinner for Maeve. Even as I thought it, I realized I didn't really care.

It was a good thing I'd gone to Bellagio's the week before and stocked the freezer. It meant a little creative thawing, but I was able to put together an acceptable dinner of chicken patties, green beans, and instant potatoes. We were limited to seltzer as a beverage. Maeve had never had flavored seltzer before and was a little skeptical.

Carefully pouring her a glass, I said, "It's something of an acquired taste. My mom drank it all the while I was growing up, so I learned to drink it. It's sort of like a soda without all the sugar and sodium. Dad orders it direct from the company in New York."

Maeve took a sip and wrinkled her nose as the bubbles tickled. "I think I could get to like it if I had a chance to acquire a taste for it. Would you mind terribly if I just drink ice water?"

Taking her glass to the sink, I rinsed it out and refilled it with ice and plain water from the tap. "I'm sorry I don't have anything else around here to drink."

Reaching out to take the glass, she assured me, "Ice water's fine, really."

After dinner we walked to the screened house at the shore end of the dock and sat on the big swing. "This is nice, isn't it?" Maeve said. "You're lucky having someplace like this to escape to."

Taking in a deep breath of the night air, I looked out over the river. "It is nice. I never thought of it as escaping, but I think you're right. River Dream is where I escape to the peace of the river."

That gave me an idea. I turned to look at her. "Maeve, I think you've just given me the name for my new boat: Riverscape. It's a play on river escape."

Maeve moved closer to me on the swing. "I think that's a wonderful name for your boat, Mike," she said as she turned her head up to me. Then in a soft voice she asked, "Now are you going to kiss me or what?"

So I kissed her. Then we kissed again. I guess we spent quite a bit of time kissing there in that swing. It was pretty late when I took her back to camp.

Eighteen

The morning after Maeve and I sailed Riverscape to River Dream, I woke up late. It wasn't a problem since I had the morning off. New camper registration wouldn't begin until around two, so I didn't need to be at camp before one. I started a pot of coffee and looked around for something to eat. Chase knocking on the door startled me. Maeve was with him.

Chase was an early riser and always seemed to be in a cheerful mood out of keeping with the time of morning. "Good morning, lazybones," he greeted me as he realized I'd just gotten out of bed.

I returned his cheerful greeting with a scornful look. "I haven't had my coffee yet."

Chase laughed and warned Maeve, "Watch out, he's a bear until he has his coffee in the morning."

"Maeve's welcome here. She's a crew member I can rely on," I said as I poured myself a cup of coffee. Maeve gave me a curious look when I went to the fridge, took out a bottle of maple syrup, and poured a healthy dose into the cup. "It's a bad habit I picked up from my dad."

"What, drinking coffee?" Maeve asked, still looking puzzled.

I dug a spoon out of the drawer where such implements were kept and stirred the syrup into the coffee. "No, the maple syrup.

Drinking coffee is a bad habit I picked up from this turkey here at Camp."

Chase folded his hands in a sign of contrition and bowed his head towards Maeve. "It's true, I must confess. I corrupted him." Maeve shook her head and laughed.

Not sure how things stood between us in light of the previous night, I thought I should proceed with caution. "How are you this morning, Maeve?" I asked as I set down my cup. Her reply was to come over and give me a hug. I embraced her tightly, perhaps for a moment too long.

Chase observed the scene with interest. "Hm, I think something more than sailing went on between you two yesterday."

"Why don't you shut up," I said crossly. Chase just grinned a satisfied little grin, and I couldn't help but grin back.

Stepping back slightly but keeping her arm around my waist, Maeve informed Chase that I cooked her a nice dinner when we got back from Oriental because she was late for dinner at camp. Chase accepted this with a nod, though his eyes showed he doubted that was the whole story. Then Maeve scolded me. "Mike, you be nice to Chase. He gave me a ride over here."

I looked at Chase for an explanation. "I planned to come over to see the new boat and asked if she wanted to come. I really had to twist her arm." Maeve gave him a sharp look until she realized he was kidding.

With only a little difficulty, I reached behind me to pick up my coffee cup. It was a little difficult because I had one arm around Maeve. "Have you two had breakfast, because I haven't."

"We had some of Miss Gladys' pancakes and sausage," Chase disclosed. "She wouldn't give us any of your real maple syrple though." Maeve chuckled at his mispronunciation of syrup.

"Good for her. Maeve may be maple worthy, but you certainly aren't. So how did your date with Liana go?"

Chase's smile was forlorn to say the least. "Quite nicely, thank you. I got a polite handshake good-night at her cabin door."

Maeve looked at me with mild panic. Did she think I'd tell Chase? I wouldn't, at least not right then and there.

Chase was pointedly staring at my coffee cup. "Pardon my manners; would either of you like some coffee?"

Maeve shook her head. "None for me, thanks." She removed her arm from my waist and sat down at the kitchen table.

Having been waiting for me to ask, Chase said, "I'd love a cup."

"You know where everything is," I told him as I went to the cabinet in hopes of finding something for breakfast.

"Some hospitality you have." He laughed and picked his cup from the collection hanging on the rack over the sink. It was actually his; he'd brought it from home. It was the only NC State mug on the rack.

Maeve laughed as she watched me go through one cereal box after another, testing to see if it was fit to eat, and throwing the box in the trash if I decided it wasn't. I finally found some that wasn't stale and poured myself a bowl.

Noticing I didn't add milk, Maeve asked, "Are you going to eat it dry?"

"Always," I said.

"Michael was traumatized by a bowl of soggy cereal when he was a child. He's eaten dry cereal ever since," Chase told her.

I finished my cereal. Chase and I refilled our coffee cups, and the three of us walked down the dock out to the lift.

"Why did you pull her out of the water?" Chase asked.

"Mostly to see if I could and partly because I don't know how long it will be until I can take her out again."

He walked around her, expertly appraising her lines. "Have you come up with a name for her yet?"

"Actually, Maeve did. She suggested Riverscape. It's a play on the words river and escape."

Chase nodded in approval. "I like it. That's very clever, Maeve."

Maeve began to protest that I came up with the name after something she said, but the look on my face stopped her. I wanted Chase to think it'd been her idea. He'd like it better that way.

Chase checked his watch and thought for a moment. "Listen, I have to go to town, Arapahoe, not New Bern. Mike, can you give Maeve a ride back to camp?"

I said a silent "God Bless You, Chase" then out loud, "Okay with me."

"Great, Maeve you don't mind, do you?"

Maeve smiled shyly. "No, I don't mind."

"All right then, I'll see you two at camp." Chase handed me his coffee cup and left.

After he was out of sight, I turned to Maeve. She threw her arms around me. "I thought he'd never leave."

"Me too either," I said. Then I kissed her. I must have looked pretty silly trying to hug her with a coffee cup in each hand. We decided to go back inside.

Once we were seated in what passed for the cottage's living room, Maeve turned serious. "Mike, can we talk about what happened last night?"

An uncomfortable feeling started to form in the pit of my stomach. "You're not having second thoughts are you, morning-after regrets?"

Her eyes widened in protest. "Oh no, God no, last night was great! There's just an aspect of this we need to talk about."

"That sounds pretty serious." The feeling in my gut faded some but lingered.

Maeve took a deep breath and seemed to be trying to decide how to say what she had to say. "I have a boyfriend back home, but we have an open relationship. What we do when we're not together is our own business. But when summer's over and I go home, I go back to him."

Not quite what I expected, but I could live with it. I wasn't looking for any kind of long-term anything. Still, I couldn't wait to see what the rest of the summer was going to be like.

The rest of the summer was pretty darn good. Maeve and I spent all our time off together, most of it on the river on board Riverscape. She spent every night in the staff cabin just like she was supposed to, but we found time to explore more than just the river.

Endless summers really aren't, and our summer love ended the August day her parents arrived to take her home. Much to my chagrin, her boyfriend was with them. Their happy reunion precluded any sentimental good-bye I'd envisioned. Seeing him I felt it best if I just sailed off into the sunset. As I rounded the corner of the camp store I heard her call my name.

"Don't think you can get away that easily, Michael. You haven't kissed me good-bye," Maeve said just a little indignantly.

Looking over her shoulder as if I expected him to follow her around the corner, I asked, "What about Roger? What would he say?"

Gently placing one hand on my cheek, she looked up at me with those enchanting heather-blue eyes. "What do I care? He'll get over it. Now come here and kiss me." I took her in my arms and kissed her thoroughly. I was going to miss her, but I knew the score going in, no regrets.

"I am going to miss you, Mike. I'm glad I got to know you," Maeve said almost in a whisper. I thought I might have seen a tear forming in those blue eyes.

She turned, walked away, rounded the corner, and was gone. I watched her go and then went to find Chase. We were taking Riverscape out one last time before we went home.

Nineteen

I'd been home from River Dream a couple of days when I felt the need to crank up my motor boat, a fourteen-foot Carolina Skiff I got the summer I turned thirteen, for a ride up the waterway. There was a lot for me to think about. As I entered the Intercoastal Waterway and turned north, I tried to imagine what senior year had in store for me.

Jill was still at her grandmother's. I didn't know what was going to happen between Jill and me, but we weren't meant to be together. My summer with Maeve proved that, even if I never was going to see her again. And what about Rhiannon? Did my feelings for Maeve mean I was finally over her?

The farther I cruised the more questions I came up with, lots of questions with no answers. At last I turned the skiff around and headed back to the dock. One of those summer storms coastal North Carolina is famous for caught me before I got home. I arrived soaking wet and still confused, hoping that when I saw Jill again things would become clear.

About nine o'clock on the last Friday morning of summer vacation, I woke up to the sound of the phone ringing. For me to be in bed so late was unusual, but I'd been out at Mikey's the night before. During our time together, Jill taught me to play guitar, and I'd played some in an informal after-hours jam session.

Still groggy with sleep, I reached for the phone. "I hope this is important."

The girl at the other end of the line didn't appreciate my salutation. "I hope you think it is," Jill replied, sounding annoyed.

She couldn't see it, but I grabbed my head and winced. "Jill, sorry, I didn't know it was you. I figured it was Hans calling to wake me up."

"Did I wake you? I'm sorry. I couldn't imagine you'd still be in bed this late." Jill sounded somewhat surprised and a little disappointed.

Squinting against the sunlight sneaking in past the edges of my blinds, I bit my lip before simply replying, "It was a late night at Mikey's last night."

With a disinterested "Oh," she asked, "can I come over?"

Thinking to myself I wasn't sure that was a good idea, I hesitated a moment before answering. "Sure, should I come get you?"

"Uh, no, that's okay. I'm actually at the pier with Rhiannon and Sabrina."

Jill was with Rhiannon. Wasn't that just cozy? "Oh, really, are they coming too?" There was perhaps a trace of annoyance in my voice.

"No, it'll just be us. Maybe we can go sailing."

Something about the way she said it suggested the idea of sailing was more for the other girls to hear than it was a serious suggestion. I played along. "Uh, yeah, I'll check the weather. It shouldn't be a problem though." Doubting we would ever get as far as the dock, I had no intention of checking the weather.

"OK, I'll see you in a few minutes," Jill said with a false note of cheerfulness in her voice.

Placing the phone gently in its cradle, I rubbed my eyes and tried to think. Jill was back in town but hadn't called to tell me until just then. She went to see Rhiannon first before she even called me. Why? Weren't Rhiannon and Sabrina at Mikey's last night? Wasn't Sabrina supposed to be leaving for college today? Jill wanted to go sailing. I figured I'd better get up and get dressed.

I'd barely pulled on my shorts when I heard Jill holler up from the deck, "Michael, are you up there?"

"I'll be right down," I called out through the screen door. Grabbing a t-shirt from the drawer, I padded barefoot down the stairs. Pulling my t-shirt over my head as I reached the bottom of the stairs, I wondered why my mom or dad hadn't let her in. When I got to the kitchen I found out why. They weren't home. There was a note on the fridge telling me they'd taken Malori to some kind of orientation at her school. I walked out onto the deck.

Forcing what I hoped looked like a genuine smile, I said, "Hi, Jill, it's good to see you," as she gave me a hug.

Her smile was just as forced. "It's good to see you too, Mike," she said as she pulled back. No kiss, just the hug. She didn't look like she was dressed for spending time on the water.

"Do you really want to go sailing?" I asked.

Looking first toward the driveway and then over my shoulder towards the house, she asked, "Are your folks around?"

Plainly she didn't want to go sailing. "No, they'll probably be gone until after lunch."

Jill looked like she was trying to make up her mind about something. Finally she suggested, "Then let's go inside and talk?"

I stepped aside and motioned for her to precede me through the door.

She sat down at the table, and I started looking for the fixings for coffee. The way I was feeling and the direction I figured things were headed in, I thought I could use a cup.

Watching me, Jill asked, "Mike, what are you doing?"

Holding up the carafe like it was a trophy, I said, "Making a pot of coffee, would you like some?"

She looked a little puzzled. She knew I knew she didn't drink coffee. "No thank you."

Having filled the coffee maker with water and the basket with grounds, I pushed the start button. "Suit yourself."

Jill's lips were drawn into a tight line. "Mike, something happened over the summer I need to tell you about."

The coffee maker started making that noise they make when the water starts to heat up. Satisfied I would have my joe shortly, I sat down across from Jill. "Okay, shoot."

Her eyes widened and her hand flew to her face. "Just like that, you want me to just blurt it out?"

I shrugged and held my hands out toward her. "If it's good news, I'll be glad to hear it, and if it's bad news, waiting won't make it any better."

"I suppose you're right." She took a deep breath and began. "Here goes. I met someone over the summer. He's just finished his freshman year as an art major at Warren Wilson College. He works at my grandmother's gallery part-time."

So it's bad news, I thought to myself. Then I reconsidered. "He sounds like a nice guy," I said with all the sincerity I could muster.

Jill smiled a real smile. "He is. His name is Rick. He reminds me of you in some ways, but in most ways he's nothing like you."

I wasn't quite sure how to take that. "Really, how so?"

Jill frowned just a little. "Well, he's not the kind of guy who'd name a star after a girl. But when I'm with him, I feel like I always hoped I'd feel with you."

While I may have been expecting regret or sadness from Jill when she said this, all I got was resignation. As for my feelings, it was all academic. I decided to be happy for her.

"Jill, if he's the man who can make you happy, then I think that's great."

Anger was not the reaction I expected. "Damn it, Mike, can't you even be a little jealous? Didn't I mean anything to you?"

"Are you kidding me? Of course you meant something to me. How did you want me to react? This is about the worst thing you could have come here to tell me."

"It's about the worst, Michael. What could have been worse, that I found out I'm gay?"

Her words were like knives in my chest. "That's a low blow, Jill," I said with quiet anger.

Tears brimmed in her eyes as she realized how hurtful those words were to me. "Oh God, Michael I'm so sorry. I am so sorry," Jill said, really starting to cry.

Her tears, sincere or not, had no effect on me. "I hope you and Rick are very happy together, Jill. I think maybe you had better go now." My words dripped with cold.

Jill leaned over the table and took my hands. "Mike, no, please, I don't want it to end this way."

I pulled my hands away and sat back in my chair. "How did you think it would end?"

Her chin dropped to her chest and she took a shaky breath. "Not like this," she said so softly I could barely hear her.

Not knowing what to say, I rose and got a cup of coffee. Leaning against the counter I turned to see her watching me, waiting for me to say something, anything. To give myself a moment to collect my thoughts, I took a careful sip. Once my emotions were under control, I said what I needed to say.

"Jill, I don't know why, but it just wasn't meant to be for us. I'm sad that's so. But truly, if Rick is the guy for you, then I'm happy for you. I wish you only happiness. It's what I always tried to give you."

The sad smile she managed almost broke my heart. "I know, Michael, and I was happy with you. We were happy. If that was enough then…but we both want love and for whatever reason we never found it with each other."

I knew the reason. I knew it only too well. Loving Jill had been impossible while I was still in love with Rhiannon. That didn't mean I didn't care. "Jill, I am going to miss you; I'll miss us."

Her smile brightened, just a bit. "Hey, I'll still be around. We do go to the same school. And I hope we can still hang out together."

Our hanging out together was not something I could see happening, but telling her so right then would've been the wrong thing to do. "Are you sure you'd be okay with that?" I asked her instead.

Jill got up from the table and took a hesitant step toward me. "I am if you are."

"I am," I lied.

She reached out and lightly touched my arm. "Good, okay, I'm glad. Now I do have to get going." I walked her to her car, and she did kiss me good-bye. It was a chaste kiss, a kiss between friends. She drove off and was gone.

Twenty

Jill hadn't been gone five minutes when someone knocked on the door. I was sitting at the breakfast table, staring into my coffee cup, trying to work out my feelings about what just happened. Though Jill and I wound up parting on friendly terms, what she'd said in reference to Rhiannon still stung. The more I thought about it the more I realized it really was because of my suppressed feelings for Rhiannon that I couldn't love Jill.

It was Rhiannon at the door. "What a surprise, I didn't expect to see you today," I told her, not knowing if I was glad to see her or not.

The look on her face said she didn't quite believe me. "I can imagine. I didn't expect to be here either. I just saw Jill drive off."

Leaving the door open behind me to indicate she should feel free to follow me inside, I headed back to the kitchen to warm up my coffee. "Yeah, she just left."

Rhiannon came in, looked at the nearly empty coffee pot, and shrugged. "How did it go?"

I held up the coffee pot as my way of asking her if she wanted a cup. She shook her head no. Setting it back on the warmer, I returned to my seat. She waited patiently while I took a sip. "It went about as well as could be expected, I guess. We parted on friendly terms. She's found someone else."

Rhiannon took the seat across from me, the one recently vacated by Jill. "I'm sorry things didn't work out." She sounded like she really meant it.

Those green eyes I'd known all my life looked back at me in sympathy when I raised my head to meet her gaze. "That's the way it goes," I said.

"Oui, mon ami. That's the way it goes."

We sat there quietly for a while, me sipping my coffee, her watching me. Rhiannon knew me well enough to know what I needed most right then was the quiet company of a good friend. Eventually my curiosity overcame my morose thoughts. "I figured you'd be spending the day with Sabrina."

Mention of Sabrina brought a sad look to her face. We were quite a gloomy pair. "No, she's leaving for Georgetown today. We had her going-away party at Mikey's last night, remember."

"Oh, yeah," I said, wincing slightly. "How are you holding up?"

She sighed and seemed to decide she wasn't going to mope about it. "I'm cool with it. I mean, we knew it was coming, so we spent as much time together as we could this summer. And she'll be home holidays and stuff. She's going to have a phone in her dorm room so we can talk now and then. It'll be okay." Then changing the subject rather abruptly, Rhiannon asked, "Have you seen Mrs. Nadeau this summer?"

Turning an expression on Rhiannon that said, duh, I've been gone most of the summer, I responded, "Kind of a funny thing to ask. Why?"

Rhiannon had turned to look out the window and didn't answer for a moment. Then she shrugged and turned back toward me. "I saw her yesterday at the store, and she asked me the funniest thing. She asked me about you."

Sensing I was being set up, I was on my guard. "What did she ask about?"

"We got to talking about school starting up and what classes I was taking. Then she asked if I had any classes with you. I told her no, and she said that was a shame. She said you were a nice young man and asked why the two of us had never gone out."

"Did you tell her?"

Hers eyes widened in mock horror. "Michael, of course not, I told her we'd been friends all our lives but didn't feel that way about each other."

You mean you don't feel that way about me, I thought to myself. Me, I would have loved for us to go out. "What did she say?"

"She said I was missing out, that you're an incredible kisser," Rhiannon said with a straight face.

"What!" I choked out as I felt the blood rising in my cheeks.

"Michael, goodness, I was just kidding. Michael!" She exclaimed, clearly becoming concerned.

For a moment I couldn't catch my breath. Finally I looked at Rhiannon. "That was most certainly not funny."

She was laughing so hard she could barely get the words out. "If you coulda seen the look on your face, you'd know it was funny, at least from where I'm sitting."

"You...if only...but..." I stuttered, shaking my head.

Rhiannon looked at me hard for a long, long moment. "Oh my God, Michael, you and Mrs. Nadeau," she said in disbelief.

Now it was my turn to put on a cat-who-caught-the-canary grin. "Gotcha," I said triumphantly.

"You, Michael, are a certified, grade A, brat," Rhiannon pronounced. "As if Mrs. Nadeau would ever," she trailed off. Yet the look on her face made me think she was wondering if just maybe it could happen. With a crooked grin and a slow shake of her head, she silently decided not.

"You never know," I said, sitting back and taking a slow, deliberate sip of my coffee, "rumor has it I'm a pretty incredible kisser."

"If you say so, you kook." She got up, and on her way to the fridge, patted my head. Looking through all the pitchers until she found the grape juice, she poured herself a glass and sat back down. We sat there for a while watching each other drink.

Finishing my coffee, I was debating with myself whether to have another. A quick look at Rhiannon's glass showed she was about done, too.

"Well, Sabrina's gone off to college and Jill's just gone. It's you and me kid. You wanna go sailing?"

Rhiannon's face lit up like a sunrise. "I thought you'd never ask."

Leaving a note for my folks telling them I'd gone sailing, and after Rhiannon called her folks to tell them, we headed down to the dock to get Hey 19 ready. Hey 19 was my West White Potter 19 foot sailboat, named after the Steely Dan song. She was easy to rig, and soon we were pointed towards the inlet on our way out to open water.

I shot the inlet under sail. It was a testament to Rhiannon's trust in my sailing skills that she didn't bat an eye at this. The sun was out in force, and I was soon down to my beach britches at the helm. Rhiannon, I soon discovered, had worn a lavender bikini under her t-shirt and shorts. The winds were from the southwest, so I put us on a starboard tack close hauled and we headed south down the coastline just outside the surf zone.

"I thought you'd sail north up the beach so you could look at all the pretty girls in their bikinis," Rhiannon teased.

Giving it right back to her I replied, "Why would I when I've got the prettiest girl on Wrightsville Beach in a bikini right here on my boat?" Though we were just kidding around, I meant every word.

Rhiannon rolled her eyes. "Nice try, Michael. I'm hardly the prettiest girl on the beach."

Serious for a moment, I looked her right in her lovely green eyes. "You always have been to me."

So help me, Rhiannon actually blushed. "Thank you, Mike," she said shyly. "Now shut up and steer the boat."

After an hour of beating down the coast, we jibed into a run for deep water, sailing wing on wing. Hey 19 seemed to be flying. That gave me an idea.

"Rhiannon, you should fly with me sometime." How it was she'd never flown with me yet when I'd been a licensed pilot for over a year puzzled me until I recalled flying was something Jill and I had learned together.

"What, in your rickety old Piper Cub?"

"She may be old, but Sky Dream isn't rickety. The guys who restored her were pros. They did a great job."

Rhiannon pretended to be contrite. "I'm sorry, Michael. I didn't mean to insult your airplane. I'd love to go fly with you sometime."

"How about tomorrow? I'm flying up to River Dream to check on the house."

The disappointment on her face wasn't pretend. "I have to work tomorrow. I have to work tonight too, now that I think about it. Maybe we'd better head in."

Reluctantly I replied, "Aye, aye, ma'am, coming about." I brought her back through the inlet under sail, and while Rhiannon didn't blink, I think a few folks on shore thought me a bit reckless.

Hey 19 never balked. I eased her up to the dock never once having used the motor coming or going. Hey 19 might not have been as sleek and fast as Riverscape, but she handled well.

Rhiannon jumped nimbly to the dock and tied off the bow line. "Thanks for the sail, Mike. Are you coming to the pier tonight?"

With a mischievous grin and raised brow, I replied, "If only to talk your dad into giving you tomorrow off so you can fly with me, I'll be there."

"Don't you dare, Michael."

Seeing she was serious, and knowing it would mean her dad having to work extra hours, I relented. "All right, we'll fly away together another time."

After going to the pier with Hans that night to fish for spot, I got up on Saturday, picked him up, and we flew to River Dream for the weekend. We spent the time fishing and sailing. Sunday afternoon it was back to Wilmington. Monday started senior year.

Twenty-one

On the first day of senior year Hans and I walked into Mr. Shumaker's home room both excited and nervous. Hans was excited, and I was nervous.

"Math this year is gonna rock," Hans announced with enthusiasm I didn't share.

"For you maybe, you're a math genius."

"Don't worry, Michael, I'll make sure you muddle through."

Hans and I were in Mr. Shumaker's home room since we were both taking college preparatory math courses. Mr. Shumaker had a Master's Degree in Applied Mathematics and taught the hard math.

As if the hard math weren't enough, Hans and I would also be taking science classes at the University of North Carolina-Wilmington. Hans got selected because of his outstanding academic achievements in math and science. Though I applied just like Hans did, I always suspected the regular donations to the university from my educational foundation swayed them in my favor.

Hans disagreed. "You're too hard on yourself, Michael. You make decent grades. Not as good as mine, maybe, but mostly A's. Donations or not, they wouldn't have picked you if they didn't think you could hack it."

As great an opportunity as the program was, it did complicate our lives in some ways. Hans and I played on the Buccaneer soccer team and would have to hightail it back to the high school for soccer practice after our college classes.

Being in the program also meant some imaginative curriculum changes to my NJROTC class work. Sophomore and junior years, I'd been a cadet. Getting all the classes I needed to graduate, and take part in the UNCW program, meant cutting NJROTC from my schedule senior year. Chief Spencer had very few seniors to fill out the officer billets and came up with a way to keep me on the rolls.

"Michael, what if I could offer you a chance to do independent study? That way you'd stay on the roster as cadet battalion logistics officer. You'd have to read some books and articles, write a few papers, inventory the supply room once a month, and run copies for me now and then."

We got the okay from the principal and the NJROTC chief advisor at Hoggard High. Completing three years of JROTC would mean enlisting in the Navy as a Seaman rather than as a Seaman Apprentice. A small distinction, but it seemed important to me at the time. Doing a hitch in the Navy before starting college was part of my plan.

While we were sitting in home room the first morning, Hans asked about Jill.

"You two have really called it quits?"

"Yeah, we're done. She met some guy out in Asheville, and I guess it's true love."

Hans nodded sympathetically. "And what about that girl, May, you met at camp? Any chance of that turning into something?"

I rolled my eyes and corrected him, again. "Her name's Maeve, and no, there's no chance. She made that clear. When we left camp we left behind whatever there was between us."

"So basically you've got no one right now, unless you count Rhiannon."

There was always Rhiannon. Things didn't get much more complicated than my friendship with Rhiannon.

"Hans, there's no me and Rhiannon. We're just friends, and friends are all we'll ever be. You should know that better than anyone."

"So you two keep saying." He didn't sound convinced.

With Jill out of my life and Sabrina off to Georgetown, Rhiannon and I wound up spending a lot of time together. People who didn't know us thought we were a couple, but the little things couples do - holding hands, kissing, the cutesy things - they were absent. We were just two friends hanging out. Hans was glad I had Rhiannon to hang out with since he and April were more on than off those days.

Summer drifted toward fall, and school days came and went. Every weekend I could I spent at River Dream, flying up Saturday mornings and home Sunday evenings. Depending on wind and weather, I'd sail Riverscape up to New Bern or down to Oriental. Some weekends Hans would go with me; some weekends Wes would. Chase even made it down from Apex now and then. I asked Rhiannon several times, but she was always busy working at the pier.

As the calendar changed to October and good fishing weather moved in, I decided I needed another boat, a fishing boat, to use at River Dream. When I brought up the idea with my dad I expected him to protest. Instead he just asked, "What kinda boat you got in mind?"

"I've been thinking about a Grady-White. They're made right here in North Carolina. Maybe a twenty-footer, something good for the Neuse and the sound."

Dad nodded. "That'd be a good size. Grady-White builds a good boat. Considering how much stock you own in Boston Whaler, it wouldn't hurt to give them a look, too."

"I own stock in Boston Whaler?"

"The trust does. So, de facto, you do. Mr. Justin knew Richard Fisher, the man who founded the company. It's not a controlling share or anything, but I'm sure if they learn you want a boat they'll expedite the request. Didn't I tell you all this when we bought your skiff?"

Since my skiff wasn't a Whaler, I wondered what that had to do with it. "You probably did, Dad. It was a few years ago."

Dad looked over the top of his glasses at me. "How soon do you want this boat?"

Knowing it was cutting things kind of close, I hesitantly said, "I'd like to take Hans and Wes fishing next weekend. You, too, if you want to come along,"

He thought about that for a moment or two. "I'll contact Grady-White and see what they can do about getting a boat delivered by then. They'll probably refer me to a dealer around Oriental somewhere. I'm sure there's one close." Then he looked up and smiled. "And yes, I'd like to go with you. It's been a while since we've done something like that together."

Good to his word, Dad told me a couple days later a fully outfitted Grady-White 200 Dolphin with a 200-horse Johnson outboard would be waiting at the Marina for us on Saturday morning. I don't know how he did it. He was good with things like that.

All four of us in the Piper Cub with our gear would have been too much, so we planned to drive up Friday night in my dad's Suburban. The house was still under construction, so we'd all bunk in the cottage. Dad would stay in my bedroom while Hans, Wes and I bunked in the second bedroom. It had two sets of bunks. My bedroom used to have the same, but I refurnished it when I moved in. I couldn't imagine eight people sharing that little cottage.

Leaving Friday after school would mean missing the football game Friday night. April and Allie weren't too happy with Hans and Wes over it. When I told Rhiannon I thought she might be a little upset we wouldn't be there to see her cheer.

"It's just one game, Mike. Why should I care if you miss one game? Go enjoy your weekend with the boys." Those were her words, but there was something about her tone I couldn't quite put my finger on. Then again, she and I weren't going out together, so why would she mind if I didn't make the game? Still it bothered me a little that she acted like it didn't bother her at all.

The one who surprised me was Beth. "What do you mean you won't be at the game?" she asked testily at lunch on Wednesday.

Recoiling from the angry look on her face, I explained. "My dad and I are taking the guys fishing. We're leaving right after school and driving up."

The hurt look in her eyes tore at my heart. "Why can't you stay for the game and fly up Saturday morning like you usually do?"

It's funny how that became matter of fact among my friends. "Sky Dream isn't big enough for the four of us and our gear."

Beth was in no mood to be reasonable. "Then I guess you need to buy a bigger airplane, don't you?"

Beth was one of my closest friends, but I couldn't understand why she got so worked up about me missing a football game.

"It's not just you, Mike; it's you, Hans, and Wes. Three of my best friends won't be there to see me...oh never mind," Beth sobbed. That made me feel really bad, but I still didn't understand why. I looked at Hans, he looked at Wes, and Wes looked at me. April and Allie were looking at us like we'd just kicked a kitten.

"To see you what Beth?" I asked her cautiously. Then it hit me. Beth had been nominated for the McDonald's All-American Band. The award was taking place at Friday's game. "I'm such an idiot.

Beth, I'm sorry, of course we'll stay for the game. We can leave after half-time."

Beth dried her eyes on a napkin. "You'd do that?" she sniffed, a hint of a smile forming.

Right then I would have offered to walk barefoot on the moon if it'd get her to stop crying. "Beth, we're your friends. We wouldn't miss your big moment for the world."

"Thanks, guys," she said, breaking into a genuine smile. "That means a lot."

April and Allie were pleased the guys were going to the game after all but weren't too pleased we'd still be leaving after half-time. Dad was cool about the change in plans and wound up going to the game with us. When I told Rhiannon, she said staying was a nice thing for us to do.

The first half didn't go well for the Buccaneers, but the half-time show and Beth's presentation were very nice. We intercepted her as she came off the field and gave her a big bouquet. She cried and hugged us before rejoining the band. Hans and Wes said good-bye to April and Allie. Then the four of us guys piled into the Suburban and headed to Pamlico County. We arrived at River Dream around midnight.

Twenty-two

Morning came too early. Forcing my eyes open, I looked around the room, wondering what woke me. Hans was just stirring in his bunk, but Wes's bunk was empty. Then I heard the voices.

"Mr. Lanier, all this really belongs to Mike?" Wes asked in low tones.

"That's right, Wes."

"I always thought it was family land or something."

"It's kind of complicated," Dad explained, "having to do with trust funds and such his godfather set up for him."

"Well, for a rich kid, Mike's an okay guy." There was a touch of humor in Wes' voice.

There was a touch of pride in Dad's voice as he said, "I'm glad you think so. His mom and I did our best."

Looking over at Hans, I saw him give me a thumbs up. Hans knew quite a bit about my peculiar situation after all the years we'd known each other. Even a kid can figure out a few things, and Hans was a very smart kid. Wes had only known me since sophomore year. There was a lot about me he didn't know. Now, thanks to my dad, he knew a little more. I didn't mind. I trusted my dad's instincts. If he thought it was okay for Wes to know, it probably was.

Getting out of bed, I visited the one bathroom and headed to the kitchen. Dad had brewed a pot of coffee and, why was I surprised, next to it sat a bottle of maple syrup. I made myself a cup and joined him and Wes on the back porch. They were watching a sailboat, spinnaker out and full, running downriver.

"It would be a nice day for a sail," Dad commented.

Gingerly I sipped my coffee. "That's not our plan for today," I reminded him. "We've got a date with some drum."

"Now that's a plan I can subscribe to," Hans said coming out behind me. I noticed he had a cup of light brown liquid that started out as coffee but was more cream and sugar than java juice.

"I like the sound of that," Wes agreed enthusiastically.

Dad took one more look at the sailboat making its way quickly by before announcing, "Then gentlemen, if you're all ready, I suggest we head to the Minnesott for some breakfast and then on to Oriental."

The Minnesott Grill was in an old convenience store near the Minnesott Ferry landing. Remodeled into a diner by its new owners, the Grill served up a great breakfast. We loaded into Dad's Suburban and headed there before going to the Marina in Oriental to pick up the new boat. Jeremy, the Marina manager, promised us it would be ready by nine. We pulled in at five minutes past.

"Michael, didn't I just deliver you a boat this summer?" Jeremy asked with a grin.

I laughed at the expression on his face. "Yes, you did, Jeremy, but that was a sailboat. I need something that'll outrun the fish."

Jeremy appraised me for a moment and then turned towards the boat. "This baby ought to do it with that big Johnson on the back. Let me give you the walk-around before we put her in the water."

As Jeremy gave us the information on the boat, we followed him around like baby ducks following their mother. He would point and we would all look. It must've been a comical sight to anyone happening by. At last Jeremy was satisfied he'd covered what he needed to, and the lift driver put the boat in the water.

Once she was secure to the dock, Jeremy took us on board and showed us all the gadgets and gizmos the boat had been outfitted with. He showed us how to start the motor and where all the important gauges and buttons were. Then he handed me the keys and wished me happy boating.

Wes and Hans played rock-paper-scissors to see who'd accompany me on the boat and who would drive with Dad back to River Dream. Wes won. Hans and Dad would stop by the bait shop and pick up some shrimp and squid. Waving good-bye, Wes and I motored out of the Marina and into the river. As we cleared the no-wake zone and I put more power to the engine, I thought of the last time I'd been there, with Maeve. I felt a moment of nostalgia for our summer together and wondered what she was doing right then.

The thoughtful expression on my face worried Wes for a moment. "Mike, is everything okay?"

His question shook me from my memories. "Huh, yeah, why do you ask?"

"You suddenly got a funny look on your face, like you'd heard or seen something. I thought maybe you noticed something wrong with the boat."

Reminded Wes wasn't that familiar with boats, I reassured him. "No, Wes, the boat is running fine, like a thoroughbred. I was just remembering my last trip out of the Marina."

He looked relieved, then became curious. "Really, when was that?"

A telling smile formed as I thought to myself it was during the Summer of Maeve. Answering his question I simply said, "This past summer when I picked up Riverscape. A girl I met at camp sailed her home with me."

"I see. I think you told us about her. Was she someone special?"

What a loaded question. Was Maeve someone special to me? "It was a summer fling. We both knew it was over when summer ended. She went home to her boyfriend, and I just went home." I could hear the tinge of regret in my voice. "Her name was Maeve. She named Riverscape."

Wes gave me a knowing look. "I'll bet you wish it was her sitting here with you instead of me."

"Actually, there's another girl," I mused wistfully. Wes gave me a peculiar look, but I chose not to elaborate. Maeve wasn't the girl I wanted sitting there; at least I didn't think she was. Shaking off those thoughts, I glanced over at Wes. "Let's open this puppy up and see what she's got." As I pushed the throttle to the stops, the boat leapt ahead, practically jumping from wave tip to wave tip. That big Johnson outboard pushed her over the water at better than 35 knots. It took us barely 15 minutes to reach River Dream. I compared that to the nearly 3 hours Maeve and I spent bringing Riverscape home. All in all I decided I'd enjoyed sailing with Maeve more.

The cypress and swamp maples along the north riverbank began to thin as we got closer to River Dream. Looking up toward the cottage, I noted the Suburban wasn't back yet. "Looks like we beat Hans and Dad back to the dock. Get ready to secure the bowline."

"I've got it," Wes called back over his shoulder. We tied the boat to the end of the dock and waited for Dad and Hans to arrive. While we waited we loaded the fishing gear aboard as well as a cooler full of seltzer and some provisions for lunch. Hans and Wes had both developed a taste for seltzer after hanging around with me. Mikey's even started serving it.

When Dad and Hans showed up a few minutes later, we got aboard and set out to find the fish. We had a pretty good day of it and caught a live well full of nice drum and a couple flounder. Darkness was descending on the river as we returned to the dock. After cleaning the fish we put all but the drum we planned to grill in the deep freeze on the back porch. Later, our bellies full, we sat around the screened room at the head of the dock and swapped stories. The next morning, after a breakfast of cereal and pop tarts, we cleaned the boat and the gear, packed the fish in ice, and headed back to Wilmington.

Twenty-three

My eighteenth birthday was celebrated with a big parade in downtown Wilmington. Several other cities and towns around the country held parades, too. That's what happens when your birthday is on Veterans' Day.

Though my birthday fell on a Saturday, and I usually spent Saturdays at River Dream, this particular Saturday my parents indicated they would really appreciate it if I spent it at home. Truth be told, I would've been rather disappointed had they not asked me to.

Mikey's closed Saturday night to host my birthday party. I felt that was a bit much, but Mom and Dad said they weren't about to have it at the house. Besides, since I owned the place I was the one losing out on the business, or so Dad informed me. When I walked in most of my friends were already there.

"Happy Birthday, old friend, Alles Gute zum Geburtstag," Hans wished me in English and German.

"Did you just call him a gerber stag?" April asked with a smile, "Happy Birthday, Mike." She hugged me and kissed my cheek.

Beth stepped up next and gave me a quick hug. "Happy Birthday, Mike." Greg nodded but said nothing.

Wes, Allie, and the other guests took their turns wishing me the same. I looked around for the one friend who hadn't. She was standing by the soda bar. I made my way over.

"Many happy returns on the day, Michael," Rhiannon said, lifting her glass, "and many more."

I'm not sure what I expected from her, but that wasn't it. "Many thanks to you for the fine salutation, Rhiannon. Mutual, I am sure," I said as formally as I could manage.

I'm not even sure what that was supposed to mean, but Rhiannon almost choked on her drink as she started to laugh. "C'mere, you," she said, reaching out to hug me. "Happy Birthday, Mike." That was more like what I hoped for. The band on the stage was ready to perform. They began to play "Lady" by Styx.

Barely releasing my hold on Rhiannon, I looked her in the eye. "Since I'm the birthday boy, you have to dance with me."

Rhiannon made no attempt to pull away. "Since it's your birthday, I suppose I could," she conceded with a dramatic sigh. We stepped onto the dance floor. Others joined us, but all I could see was Rhiannon. My heart was pleading for the words of the song to reach her.

All too soon the song ended, and she retreated to our gang's usual table. I wanted to follow her, but Beth was there waiting for her birthday dance. Before the party was over I danced with every female there, including my sister, Malori, and my mother. The college girl working the soda bar and the waitress, who went to Hoggard High, even danced with me, but I didn't get another dance with Rhiannon.

Twenty-four

Thanksgiving came and went. Before I knew it, Christmas was upon us. The first night of Christmas break I felt restless, so I decided to take a walk on the beach. It was a cool evening, so I slipped on my leather jacket and a hat. No destination in mind, I just felt like getting out of the house for a bit. Walking north, I'd just passed under Lumina Pier when I noticed someone sort of staggering down the beach in my direction. As she got closer I realized it was Rhiannon. She appeared to be drunk. I ran to her.

Coming to an unsteady stop she stuttered, "Well, hello there Mike ole buddy ole Buccaneer pal oh mine."

"Rhiannon, what in the world?" I was astounded seeing her in that condition.

She smiled a crooked smile and wavered unsteadily. "Whatsa matter Mike ole buddy, aren't ya glad ta see me?"

Already knowing the obvious answer, I asked the question anyway. "Rhiannon, are you drunk?"

Her smile disappeared, and she leaned toward me belligerently. "What so...so...what so...so what if I am..."

I reached out and took her by the arm. "Come on, Rhiannon, let me take you home."

Pulling her arm free, she stumbled and sat down abruptly in the sand. "NO! I don't want to gho, go, go home. I wanna stit, sit down right here."

I looked at her and then up at the sky. Not a single cloud blocked the stars. Only the lights from the pier dimmed their glory. Such clear skies promised a cold night. Sitting down next to her on the sand I asked, "What's wrong, Rhiannon?"

She was staring out at the ocean. We sat there for a while watching the waves break in the light reflected from the pier. "She broke up with me, Mike," Rhiannon finally said with a sniffle.

"I'm sorry, honey." I realized she meant Sabrina.

"And the worst part is she broke up with me for a guy," Rhiannon said somewhat angrily, kicking at the sand. "Can you believe it?"

Turning my head just enough so I could see her face out of the corner of my eye, I said softly, "No, honey, I can't."

"Well, believe it," Rhiannon growled. "You know what she said?"

"No, honey, I don't," I said, shaking my head slowly.

"She said what we'd had was a silly school girl game, that's what she said. She said it was never real. She's the one who talked me into...who told me that you would never...how could I have been so stupid?"

She wasn't making much sense, but I knew she was hurting. "I'm so sorry, Rhiannon."

She began to shiver. I took off my jacket and wrapped it around her, then put my arm around her and drew her close. She put her head into my shoulder and cried. I stroked her hair and told her it was okay to cry. I told her I was there for her and wasn't going anywhere. I whispered to her that I loved her. My heart was breaking for her.

Finally her sobs tapered off. She wiped her eyes and looked up at me. "I've always loved this jacket, Michael. It looks so good on you."

"I like it better on you," I said with a grin.

She managed a weak smile and laid her head back against my shoulder. "She's sleeping with him, that guy she met at college. They're moving in together next semester. She says she loves him." Her voice was tinged with cynicism. "I guess I was a fool."

A cool breeze from off the water caused her to wrap her arms more tightly around herself. I tightened my arm around her. "No, honey, she's the fool to have hurt you."

She turned her head and looked up at me. Rhiannon stared at me for a long time. I don't know what she saw on my face, but it was as if she read all the feelings I had for her written there.

"You love me don't you, Mike," Rhiannon said. It was a statement, not a question.

"I've always loved you, Rhiannon," I answered her truthfully. There was no hesitation, no doubt.

She looked into my eyes as if searching. "If I asked you to, would you make love to me, Michael?"

A cold fist gripped my heart as it pleaded silently, oh, Rhiannon, please don't ask me that now. I raised my eyes to the stars and then looked out to sea. The wall I built around my feelings for Rhiannon crumbled with a crash so loud I thought she must have heard it. What I did next was the hardest thing I had ever had to do.

"Rhiannon, I've loved you for as long as I can remember, but tonight I would have to tell you 'no,' I would not make love to you. I'm sorry." My voice became a hoarse whisper. "Ask me again tomorrow, next week, any other time, but not tonight. It wouldn't be right. Please don't ask me tonight."

Again, she stared in to my eyes. I felt the tears welling there, spilling down my cheeks. She reached up and caught a tear. "My dear, dear Michael, thank you. If I never find anyone else to love me, I'll always know I was loved more deeply than most people could ever hope for." She stood then and reached down to help me up. Handing me my jacket she said, "I think I'm ready to go home now."

Fear that if I let her walk away I might never see her again filled me. "I'll walk with you."

Rhiannon smiled a gentle, reassuring smile. She reached out and put a hand over my heart. "No, Mike, please, I'll be alright."

"But..." I didn't want to let her go.

She held a finger to her lips to shush me. A faint gleam sparked in her eyes. "It'll be okay, Mike. I'll see you tomorrow."

Seeing that small spark made me feel a little better. "If I can't walk you, at least I can stand here and watch you home."

That made her smile, and seeing her smile I thought maybe everything would be all right.

"Okay, Mike. I'll see you tomorrow," Rhiannon repeated. Then she hugged me, kissed my cheek, and walked to her house. I watched her until she went inside before heading home.

Unable to sleep, I lay awake for hours thinking about Rhiannon, worrying about her. Finally I fell into a fitful doze to the sound of rain starting to fall on the roof. Remembering the stars, I wondered idly when the rain moved in. What I dreamed of escaped me, but I woke up reaching for someone and feeling incredibly alone when there was no one there.

Twenty-five

Stumbling from bed into a pair of sweats, I went out on my deck to work out. Faint memories of hearing rain sometime during the night almost changed my mind, but I decided to anyway. Bright clear skies greeted me. I wondered if I imagined the night's storm. Regardless, it was a crisp, fresh morning. As the cool clean air filled my lungs, I felt renewed. Warming up as I worked out, by the time I finished the last of my daily dozen, I was a new man. I hit the shower and then headed down to find some breakfast.

The mouth-watering aroma of my mother's scrambled eggs and bacon greeted me at the top of the stairs. Seeing me enter the kitchen, Mom said with just a trace of sarcasm, "Well, Michael, I see you finally decided to join us."

Dad looked at me over the top of his paper. "We were beginning to think you were going to sleep the day away." I noticed he was still in his robe and slippers.

"It's not that late; it's only a little after eight."

Not to be left out, Malori added, "Michael's a lazy bones." Six-and-three-quarter-year-old Malori, don't forget the three-quarters thank you very much, never missed a chance to pick on her big brother.

Noting that she was still in her pajamas, I asked, "How long have you been up Mal?"

Mom turned and gave me a stern look. "Michael! I have asked you not to call her that."

"But I like him to call me that," Malori said with an indignant pout.

"Well, I do not," Mom said, turning back to the stove, effectively cutting off any further discussion.

Upsetting my mother was not a smart way to start the day. "I'm sorry, Mom." With a wink at Malori, I asked, "What time did you get up, squirt?" Dad chocked back a chuckle. Mom harrumphed but said nothing more.

"I was up early 'nough to see Rhi-nanen when she dropped off the note," Malori informed me with an imperious smile.

"Malori, her name is Rhiannon," Mom scolded without turning around.

That erased Malori's smile. "I'm trying."

Learning Rhiannon had already been by was something of a shock. "Rhiannon left me a note?"

Dad shuffled through his newspaper. "She stopped by to see you, but I told her you were still sleeping. She thought that was quite funny, by the way. She wrote you a note. I have it here someplace."

Dad found the note under his newspaper. Rhiannon had folded it up with a little tuck so no one could read it. Not quite sure if I wanted to read it, I unfolded it slowly and carefully.

Mike,

Meet me on the pier as soon as you get your lazy butt out of bed. There's something I want to talk over with you. Don't be too long or I'll catch all the fish.

Rhi

Dad was once again looking at me over the top of his paper. "May I infer from your silly grin, Michael, that it's good news?"

Tapping the note thoughtfully, I said, "Well, you know Dad, maybe it is. I've got to go."

"Michael, at least have some breakfast first," Mom said to my back as I headed out the door.

I didn't know what Rhiannon wanted to talk to me about, but I knew she was all right because of three things in the note. First, she called me a lazy butt, or called my butt lazy. If she was insulting me at that hour of the morning, she must be in a good mood. Second, she was going fishing. The one thing we did together most often besides sailing was go fishing. Third, she had signed it "Rhi." No one I knew ever dared call her Rhi except me, and that was when we were little kids. She signed the note "Rhi" to remind me we'd been friends a long time.

I stopped running as I got to the pier house steps. There weren't many people there as it was December and it was a brisk morning. Only the diehards who fished every day showed up on a day like that. I thought Han's mom would probably be out sometime later. Thinking about his mom reminded me I was supposed to call Hans first thing. He'd understand, I told myself.

Rhiannon's father was at the counter when I walked in. He smiled and motioned me over. "Michael, Rhiannon's waiting for you out on the pier. She said you two had a fishing date this morning. Are you running late or something?"

Still trying to catch my breath, I managed to reply, "Actually, Uncle Lind...I just found out...about our date. Rhiannon must have forgotten...to tell me about it...when I saw her last night."

"About last night, Michael, I want to thank you for being there to watch out for Rhiannon. I was never happy about her and Sabrina, you know that. She's my baby girl after all. Last night when Rhiannon got home, I was so worried." He paused and looked at me as if expecting me to say something.

"But she's okay this morning?" I asked, not sure what it was he was waiting for me to say.

Uncle Lind nodded slowly. He turned and noticed the pot on the coffee warmer was empty. As he prepared to make a fresh pot, he continued talking. "I think she did a lot of thinking last night." He pressed the button to start the water flowing into the basket of grounds. "She told me that you arrived like her guardian angel last night. I want to thank you for that, Michael."

"You already have," I reminded him gently.

He smiled a patient smile. "I know you love her, Michael. Deep inside I think she loves you too, she just…well, you better get out there before she decides you're not coming. I'll bring you out some coffee once the new pot is done."

I tried to think of something profound to say. "Thanks, Uncle Lind," was all I could come up with.

Cold wind hit me as I walked out onto the pier. I realized I wasn't very well prepared for a fishing date. I didn't have my rod and reel or any tackle. Shaking my head, I thought to myself, who ever heard of a fishing date anyway? When I saw Rhiannon sitting there with the sun on her hair, the way she was profiled against the bright blue December sky, I forgot all about fishing.

Sensing my approach, Rhiannon turned and frowned at me. "It's about time you got here. If you're lucky there might be one or two fish left."

Holding my hands out in a gesture of surrender, I admitted, "I didn't even bring a rod."

Rhiannon let out an exasperated sigh and shook her head sadly. "What kind of guy shows up for a fishing date without a rod and reel?"

Trying to keep a straight face, I told her, "I wasn't sure of the proper etiquette. When a girl invites you on a fishing date, does she provide the tackle or should you bring your own?"

"Since I know you so well, Michael, I knew once you read the note you'd probably run right over here without bothering to put on a jacket, much less grab your rod and reel. That's why I grabbed one for you from the rentals." She pointed to the stout casting rod and reel combo leaning against the rail next to hers.

I dared a small smile. "You know me too well, Rhiannon. So, are we really on a date?"

Rhiannon pursed her lips thoughtfully before replying. "You've always been bugging me to go on a date. Will this do?"

"It'll do for starters."

"Don't push your luck, Mike," she warned, but laughed as she said it.

I took the rod she offered, baited the hooks, and cast out as far as I could. Then I took a seat next to her on the bench, set the rod against the rail and sat back. For a while we just fished, neither of us talking.

I thought about how many hours we'd spent just like that, sitting together on the pier fishing. Sometimes we'd talk about anything and everything, but sometimes we'd just sit quietly, content with each others' company. At that moment I was quite content just to be in Rhiannon's company.

Her dad eventually arrived with the coffee. "Michael, here is the coffee I promised. You do take it black, don't you?"

Rhiannon cast me a disapproving glance. "You stopped to talk to my dad on your way out here. No wonder you were so late."

"Michael and I had a chance to catch up a bit. It's not like I get to see him every day these days, not like when you were little," Uncle Lind said, coming to my defense.

"Thanks for the coffee, Uncle Lind, black's just the way I like it." This was mostly true. When I was somewhere that didn't have maple syrup handy, I just drank it black. They didn't have maple syrup at the pier.

Rhiannon smiled sweetly at her father and asked, "Did you bring any for me, Daddy?"

"Since when did you start drinking coffee?" Lindsey asked.

"It's a day for new things," she announced. "Mike, may I try some of your coffee?"

I looked at her dad and he just shrugged. I handed her my coffee cup. "Be careful, it's very hot."

She gingerly took a sip, wrinkled her nose, and swallowed hard. "Ugh, how can you guys stand to drink that stuff?" She handed me back my cup.

Her dad laughed at the face she made. "Rhiannon, I'll go make you a nice cup of hot chocolate, okay?"

"Yes, Daddy, please, that would be very nice," Rhiannon said, all sugar and spice. Uncle Lind went back down the pier. Rhiannon looked at me and wrinkled her nose again. "How do you drink that stuff, Mike?"

Taking a careful sip, I savored the warmth before telling her, "Years of practice. You shouldn't have tried black coffee first. You might like it the way Hans drinks it. He loads it up with cream and sugar. His coffee is more a light tan than black."

Rhiannon shook her head doubtfully. "I think I'll stick to hot chocolate, thank you."

She turned her attention back to her rod. The fish didn't appear to be biting, but I thought I'd check my bait. Sure enough, the hooks were bare. I reached into the bait bucket for a couple more pieces of shrimp.

"Mike," Rhiannon said quietly, without taking her eyes off her rod.

I carefully broke off a small piece of shrimp to put on my hook. "Yeah, hon," I replied absently.

As my attention was on not sticking myself with the hook, I almost missed the little smile that flickered across her face. "There, you did it again," Rhiannon said.

Puzzled, I looked up to see what she meant. "I did what?"

"You called me 'honey.'"

"Actually, I think I said 'hon.'" Both hooks baited, I cast my line back out.

"Mike," Rhiannon said again.

I turned to look at her. "Yes, Rhiannon."

She turned to me and said, "Don't read too much into this, but I kind of like it when you call me honey."

Try as I might, I couldn't think of many occasions when I'd done that. "Really, I don't recall saying it very often."

She waited until I met her gaze before continuing. "I don't think you ever did, before last night. Last night you said it over and over."

"I did?" I asked as if it was news to me.

"Michael Justin Lanier, I wasn't as drunk as you think I was. I heard every word you said," Rhiannon told me forcefully, then softly, "every word."

I swallowed hard when she said "every word." Making sure she was looking at me, I prepared to tell her I meant everything I'd said. She beat me to the punch. "I heard you when you said you love me, nothing else that happened matters. I heard that."

I didn't know how I was supposed to react. What did she mean, 'nothing else that happened matters'?

"Michael, I said before it's a day for new things. But there's one old thing I want to hold on tight to - you." When I started to speak she cut me off. "No, Michael, let me finish."

She took a deep breath, looked out over the ocean, and continued. "I've known you all my life. Since you were old enough to see me as a girl and not just another kid, it seems you have been trying to get me to go out with you. Back then it didn't seem I was ready for the boyfriend/girlfriend thing."

Rhiannon paused, but I stayed quiet.

"Then we started high school and you met Jill. Suddenly you looked at her the way you had only looked at me. It hit me like a ton of bricks. When I saw how much she liked you, I wondered why I didn't like you like that. Then I met Sabrina and she…"

Rhiannon swallowed hard. For a minute I thought she was going to cry. No, she wanted to finish.

"I shouldn't blame her; I let myself be led willingly. It seemed to explain so much. Plus it was naughty and rebellious. And it gave me a reason for why I let you get away. Of course I couldn't be with you, I was a lesbian." Rhiannon laughed a rueful laugh.

Seeing Uncle Lind coming from the pier house, I whispered, "Here comes your dad with your hot chocolate."

She nodded, sniffed, and turned toward shore. "Goodness, daddy, what took you so long?"

Uncle Lind made an indignant grunt. "Well, my help is gone on a fishing date with some guy, so I have to work the counter all alone. Sorry it took so long."

Rhiannon answered with a smile and a hug. "I love you, Daddy. Thanks for the hot chocolate."

Uncle Lind shook his head in frustration. "Sure, you love me when I bring you the hot chocolate. You two having any luck?"

Glancing at my thus-far-undisturbed rod, I told him, "Nothing's biting."

"But we are very lucky. Lucky to be here together," Rhiannon said looking over at me.

Shivering as a cold gust tugged at his jacket, Uncle Lind said, "I need to get back inside. You two don't stay out here too long in this wind." With that he left us alone and went back inside.

Sitting down on the bench, I checked my rod tip once more before asking Rhiannon why she was telling me all that. She replied, "I did a lot of thinking last night after I left you standing there on the beach. I tried to understand why I couldn't see that...that the way you felt about me was something more than teenage infatuation. I mean I knew you liked me. You even told me several times you loved me. I thought it was flirtation. It wasn't, was it, Michael?"

Past the lump forming in my throat, I managed to say, "No, Rhiannon, it wasn't, not ever, not then, not now."

Rhiannon closed her eyes and rolled her head back. "I know that now, a little late to figure it out I suppose, but last night I finally figured it out."

I felt like I was balancing on the edge of a knife. I wasn't sure where she was going with this. Fear and hope competed inside me.

Her sudden change of subject took me by surprise. "Michael, there were girls who would've gone out with you if you'd asked, but you didn't. Well, you did ask Beth out," Rhiannon amended.

"I only asked Beth after you had turned me down, again," I reminded her.

"Yeah," she laughed, "I guess that's true." Then she turned more serious, "But you didn't ask any of the others. Why did you ask Jill?"

How could I explain that to her? After a moment's careful consideration, I decided on the plain truth. "Because I thought you'd never say 'yes.'"

That was the plain truth. Then I added, "You, Beth, and Hans all seemed to think I should. I won't lie about it, I did like her, and she clearly liked me." I stopped and took a deep breath. "But mostly because I thought you'd never say 'yes.'"

"That's what I thought. That's what I was afraid of," Rhiannon said sadly. "When I saw you kissing Jill that day at lunch, I didn't know what to think. So I let you think I was happy for you."

"Rhiannon, you must know I never loved Jill. Jill knew it. And she knew I couldn't love her because I love you."

Rhiannon bit her lip, and I saw tears forming in her eyes. "I know, Michael. I understand now."

"Sweetheart, that's all water under the bridge. I know that's cliché, but that's what it is. Jill's gone, Sabrina's gone, and we remain. The question is where we go from here." There, I'd said it. Now I would have to live with what happened next.

"That's what I wanted to talk to you about," Rhiannon said.

I sat there expectantly, but she didn't say anything for a while. After getting all that off her chest, I think she was taking a moment to decide how to say what she planned to say next. I checked my bait again. Sure enough, it was gone. I replaced it, cast again, and waited.

"Michael, would you still like to date me?" Rhiannon asked in a voice so soft the wind nearly took the words away before they reached my ears. Time stopped for me. The waves stopped on their march to the shore, the breeze stopped blowing, and my heart stopped beating. "Understand we'll have to take it slow. Too much has happened to us and between us to jump in with both feet," she continued.

So help me, tears filled my eyes. I kept expecting to wake up. A sudden cold gust hit me, and I knew it was no dream. "Yes, Rhiannon, I would like to date you," I said as I choked back the tears.

"Good," she said. And suddenly she was in my arms and holding on to me like she was drowning. She was crying. I was crying. It was ridiculous. "Good," she said again. "I was so afraid."

Now that I had her in my arms, I wasn't going to let her go. "What were you afraid of, honey?" I said into her ear as I kissed her cheek.

A shiver ran through her that had nothing to do with the cold air. "I love it when you call me 'honey.'" Rhiannon smiled. Then, more seriously, "I was afraid you'd say no."

I tightened my arms around her. "Rhiannon, Rhiannon, how could you ever fear that? I'm your Michael. I always have been. I always will be. I love you."

She pressed her head tightly against my chest. "My Michael, my Michael, I love you, too. Oh God, yes I do. I love you, too," Rhiannon said softly to my heart.

Eventually we regained our composure and sat back down on the bench, this time with my arm tight around her shoulder. We didn't give the lines another thought.

Our peaceful moment didn't last though. "So this is where you are, Michael," Hans scolded me. "And who's this girl with you who looks so much like Rhiannon only I know isn't Rhiannon because Rhiannon would never sit with you like that?"

Rhiannon laughed and snuggled tighter against me. "He did that all in one breath."

Feeling bad about not having called him, I didn't feel bad enough not to laugh along with her. "It's all the opera practice he does in the shower."

Hans hand flew to his mouth. He pretended to be scandalized. "Michael, you were never supposed to tell anyone about that." He began to laugh along with us.

I did owe him an apology. "Hans, I'm sorry I didn't call. I got invited on an early date and wound up here fishing with Rhiannon."

Rhiannon nudged me lightly in the ribs and gestured with a nod of her head towards the rail. "Watch it, you. It's a long way down to the water."

Hans looked in confusion from one of us to the other. "What's with you two this morning?"

Rhiannon kissed me on the cheek before turning a bright smile on Hans. "Hans, did you know Michael here is in love with me?"

Hans looked at her as if to say 'is that all?' "I've known since he was three years old."

"Ah, yes, but did you know I'm in love with Michael?"

"Really, and just when did this happen?" The amused look on his face told us he always believed this day would come.

"I always have been." She turned from Hans to look into my eyes. "It just took me some time and trouble to figure it out."

It might not sound like it, but we did take it slow after that. Rhiannon still had to work her shifts at the pier, so I wound up spending a lot more time there. Uncle Lind put me to work once he realized I was going to be hanging around anyway.

Twenty-six

Jill came back from Asheville at the end of Christmas break, but I didn't see her until school started back up. It got ugly the day she found out Rhiannon and I were a couple.

"Well, this is certainly a surprise," Jill said angrily. "I thought she was gay."

Her anger surprised me. Trying to remind her that she was the one who found someone else first, I retorted with, "So, how's Rick?"

She grunted out, "He's fine." Then in an ugly tone asked, "Have you slept with her yet?"

"That's really none of your business," I replied, becoming defensive and a little angry myself.

"I thought not," Jill said with a satisfied sneer. "Well I hope the two of you are very happy together."

Her attitude was setting off my temper. "I don't know what you're so upset about. You're the one who came back from summer break all involved in a new relationship." I conveniently ignored my time with Maeve.

"Let's see, Mike, you're now dating the girl the love of whom kept you from loving me. She was a lesbian, but now she's not. How dare you expect me to be happy for you? It was nice knowing you, Michael." Jill walked away without another word, and after that it was as if my friends and I didn't exist to her. Not that it bothered me much. I was finally with Rhiannon.

Rhiannon and I had our first solo date the night of the NJROTC Ball. No limo and pearls this time. Knowing what color gown she planned to wear, I bought her a lavender rose corsage. We rode to the Ball in my GTO. Rhiannon wore a simple off-the-shoulder lavender gown that shaded more toward blue. It looked good with my dress uniform.

We enjoyed every minute we were there. It may have been my imagination, but even the meal seemed better than I remembered. For the last dance I convinced the DJ to play "Lady" by Styx.

"This sounds familiar," Rhiannon commented with a coy smile.

"Really," I said innocently as I led her to the dance floor. "I don't know why."

Making our first Valentine's Day as a couple special was important to me. When I picked her up for school that morning, she found a single red rose waiting for her on the passenger seat of my GTO. In her locker she found another. A third waited on her desk in home room. She began to realize I'd enlisted some help.

Throughout the day, each time she opened her locker or reached her desk in class, there was another rose. By the time we rode home she had an eleven-rose bouquet. "Okay, Michael, how did you do it?" she asked as I held the car door for her.

I smiled innocently but said nothing. She looked into the car and saw the twelfth rose. Her breath caught in her throat as a tear fell from her eye. Carefully picking up the final rose, she added it to the others and turned to me.

"Michael," she began. I pressed my finger to her lips. "Happy Valentine's Day, honey," I said softly. Reaching up to brush her hair back, I pulled her towards me for a lingering kiss. My goal had been to make the whole day special for her. By the enthusiasm with which she returned the kiss, I'd succeeded.

Twenty-seven

Rhiannon's eighteenth birthday arrived the first Saturday in March. Her family and mine celebrated it together with our friends at Mikey's on Friday night. That night we danced nearly every dance together.

Saturday morning Dad and I picked her up and headed to the airport. Rhiannon was finally flying with me to River Dream for the weekend, but we would have a chaperon. Dad was meeting with the house contractor to go over the final stage of construction.

We arrived at the airport around nine in the morning. Flying time to River Dream was about an hour, including take off and landing. We got there a little after ten. It was a clear day, so Rhiannon could enjoy the view as we made our final approach over the Neuse River.

The Jeep didn't start on the first try, and I feared the battery was too far gone, but it cranked on the second try. We drove past the house, which was nearly finished, to the cottage. I had flown up the week before to get it ready for her.

"It's hard to believe this is the first time you've been to River Dream," I said to Rhiannon.

Rhiannon, standing next to the cottage and looking out over the river, replied, "I've heard you talk so much about it that it seems like I've been here."

"You're here now, that's the important thing." I opened the door and carried our bags inside.

Her bags went into the master bedroom while dad put our stuff in the bunk room. That done, we rejoined Rhiannon in the living room, though calling it a living room was giving it too much credit. There was a sofa, a chair, a little table, and a television. Rhiannon stood just inside the doorway.

"Michael, it's such a cute little place," Rhiannon commented as she walked through the small living room and into the kitchen. "It's a perfect little cottage, Michael."

Not having the heart to tell her its days were numbered, I motioned toward the back door. "Would you like to see the dock?"

With a couple quick steps she was right beside me. "I'd love to, Mike."

Dad stayed in the cottage while we walked over to the dock. I felt a moment of guilt as we went through the screened room and Rhiannon sat on the swing where Maeve and I made out. Taking her hand, we walked down the dock to Riverscape.

Rhiannon appraised the sail boat with a critical eye. "She's a little different from Hey 19, isn't she?"

"Yes, she is. She's a Mariner."

Rhiannon nodded as she continued to examine Riverscape. "Will we be able to take her out?"

"I think so. The weather forecast looks good." We stood there looking out over the river. I thought surely my heart would burst inside my chest. My Rhiannon was finally with me at River Dream. Gently I pulled her to me and took her in my arms. I pressed my lips to hers and kissed her deeply and passionately. She returned my effort eagerly.

"Rhiannon, I love you," I said to her softly.

"I love you, Michael," she told me as she looked up into my eyes. Then she raised her head and kissed me ever so gently.

"I've imagined this moment for so long," I confided to her, "but I never dreamed it could feel this wonderful." We stood there holding each other for I don't know how long before I heard my dad coming down the dock.

As he approached we reluctantly separated. "Rhiannon, how would you like a tour of Michael's house?" Dad asked.

Rhiannon looked at me to see how I felt about it. I smiled and nodded. "We can wait until tomorrow to go sailing," I said as I took her hand and led her back up the dock.

Rhiannon was enchanted by the house. "How soon will you be able to move in?"

Dad answered for me. "We hope to find out this weekend. It's been a work in progress since summer. If all goes well, it should be done by the end of May."

Looking back at the house from the road, Rhiannon asked, "Why's it taken so long?" That was a fair question.

"Michael wanted a lot of special things built into the house," Dad explained. "He wanted to be ecologically responsible but still have a roomy house that could stand up to a big storm."

"That required some special design and engineering," I filled in.

Rhiannon took my hand and pulled me to her, kissing me on the cheek. "I think it's just wonderful."

"I'm glad you think so," I said putting my arm around her. "Someday it will be our home."

She beamed at me but said nothing. I kissed her lightly on the lips, and she chuckled.

"Your dad's standing right there," she said nodding towards him.

"Oh, don't mind me," Dad remarked in a voice that said we should remember he was there. Rhiannon and I laughed.

Noting the sun almost directly overhead, I suggested it must be about lunch time. "Indeed it is," Dad agreed, looking at his watch. "The contractor is meeting me here at two. How's the Minnesott Grill sound?"

"It sounds great to me." Turning to Rhiannon I said, "I think you'll like it. And maybe we'll be back in time to go sailing today after all."

It was not to be. The weather turned on us while we were at lunch. It was a good thing I hadn't taken the doors off the Jeep yet. As it was, we got soaked running from the Jeep to the cottage. Cold air flowed in with the rain. After we'd changed clothes, Dad went up to the house to meet the contractor. Rhiannon and I curled up on the couch and tried to watch television.

"This isn't quite how I hoped we'd spend the weekend," I lamented.

"This is just fine with me," Rhiannon assured me as she snuggled tighter against me.

I smiled and kissed her gently on the forehead. By the time Dad returned from his meeting, we were both sound asleep. He let the door close with a bang, and we woke with a start, a little embarrassed he'd found us snoozing.

Dad plopped down in the old recliner with a satisfied smirk on his face. "Mike, good news, everything is on schedule, and the house should be ready for occupancy by graduation."

"Great news," I said as I tried to rise from the couch.

Rhiannon wasn't quite ready to relinquish her hold on me, though. She stretched and yawned. "Sorry, Uncle Owen. I guess we fell asleep."

Dad shook his head in mild amusement. "Not much else to do on a rainy afternoon like this."

Sitting up straight and taking a somewhat confused look around, Rhiannon asked, "What time is it anyway?"

With the back rest reclined and the foot rest up, Dad looked like he was ready for a little nap himself. "It's time for the two of you to cook me some dinner."

The two of us did just that. After supper, the rain let up but not the wind. Rhiannon and I bundled up and walked to the end of the dock to watch the chop on the river. Standing there watching the broken clouds scooting across the darkened sky, I noticed the darker blot of another bank of storms moving in from the southwest.

"I don't think the storm is done with us."

Rhiannon followed my gaze. A gust of wind caused her to shiver, and she clung to me tighter. "Do you think we'll be able to go sailing tomorrow?"

"I guess we'll have to wait and see." When it finally got too dark to see much, we headed back inside to find my dad had popped some popcorn and made hot chocolate.

"I thought you guys could use a little something to warm you up."

Rhiannon gave him a grateful smile as she took her mug. "Thanks, Uncle Owen."

"Yeah, thanks, Dad," I echoed, taking mine.

The three of us sat in the tiny living room trying to watch the old black and white television. Dad finally rose from the recliner, said good-night, and headed for the bunk room. Rhiannon and I stayed up a bit longer, listening to the sounds of the wind and rain. We were reluctant to leave the couch, but eventually Rhiannon rose and went to the bedroom, and I made my way to my bunk.

We woke to the sound of a storm blowing itself out over the river. As the first one up, I took it upon myself to cook us a breakfast of pancakes and bacon. Whether it was the aroma of frying bacon or fresh brewed coffee that lured Dad out, he didn't say.

Rhiannon was not so reticent. "That bacon smells wonderful, Mike. Who ever knew you could cook?"

Since I often filled in as a short-order cook at the pier, I gave her one of those what-you-talking-about looks. That caused her to smile a wicked little smile before putting her arms around me for a good morning hug. Dad made a fatherly noise from behind his coffee cup; his way of reminding us we weren't alone.

"Good morning, Uncle Owen," Rhiannon said sweetly as she moved to his chair to hug him as well. Apparently she'd slept well the night before, despite the rain or perhaps because of it, and was in a fine mood.

When we finished cleaning up from breakfast, we noticed the sun breaking through the clouds. Dressed for cold weather sailing, Rhiannon and I headed down to the dock. Dad elected to stay warm and dry in the cottage.

I got Riverscape into the water, and we motored out of the lift, hoisted the sails, and beat upwind toward Cherry Branch. Riverscape's bow cut through the choppy waves being pushed before a stiff westerly breeze. We sailed past Camp Riversail, which was still closed for the winter, and on past Camp Sea Gull. The empty mooring posts and bare docks of the two camps gave the river a lonely feel.

Clearing Minnesott Beach we came about and went on a down-river run towards Great Neck Point. Rhiannon took the helm on the run as we sailed wing-on-wing. Riverscape bounced over the choppy waves instead of crashing into them.

It was quite a ride, but Rhiannon and I had sailed together in rougher seas. Glancing back at her from my position manning the jib sheet, I saw her face aglow with the excitement of letting the boat run for all she was worth. Even all bundled up in the cold weather gear and life jacket, I thought she looked beautiful. It was what I'd waited so long for, to be sailing on this river with Rhiannon, my love. That was my real River Dream.

After nearly an hour's run we reached Great Neck Point and came about, heading back to my dock. We didn't speak much while we were out on the water; there wasn't much that needed to be said. Sailing had always been our special way to spend time together. Striking the sails as we closed the last few yards, I pushed the tiller hard over and brought Riverscape alongside the dock where my dad waited to grab the line. With his help Riverscape was quickly secured back in her lift. Once we were back in the cottage, I put some water on for tea. To give us a few minutes alone together, Dad offered to take the bags up to the airstrip and then come back for us.

A sharp whistle from the tea kettle let me know the water was ready. Two mugs were waiting with our teabags and fixings already in them. Orange-Pekoe and a touch of honey was Rhiannon's preferred blend. I steeped a cup of Earl Grey, with one sugar, for myself. Sitting down beside her on the couch, I gingerly sipped my tea.

Her auburn hair, tousled by the wind, hung loosely around her face. There was a sparkle in her green eyes. "When we decided to come here this weekend, I never dreamed it would be so special. Even with all the rain, and your dad chaperoning, it was still wonderful being here with you."

Hearing her say that warmed me in a way the tea couldn't. "We waited a long time for this, honey. It was worth the wait."

Setting her mug carefully on the low table, she moved into my arms. "If only it hadn't taken me so long to realize I love you, Michael. All that wasted time…"

Brushing the hair back from those green eyes, I kissed her gently on the lips. "It wasn't wasted, Rhiannon. The wait only made this weekend more special than it would've been."

She hugged me tighter, and her voice caught in her throat as she said, "Michael, you are such a wonderful, patient man. Why did it take me so long to realize that I've always loved you? It wasn't until you started going out with Jill that I understood."

"Understood what, honey?"

"I finally understood my love for you was so much a part of me that I didn't even recognize it until it was too late," Rhiannon said, making a face and shaking her head. "Then you were with Jill and I didn't know what to do. I'd lost you."

Taking her face in both hands, I gently lifted her head. "You hadn't lost me, honey, I was just misplaced for a while. Now I'm right where I should be."

Tears filled her eyes. "Will you love me forever, Michael?"

"I will love you until the day after forever, Rhiannon," I promised as I bent to kiss her. I don't know how far that kiss would have gone if Dad hadn't come back through the door right then.

Pointedly looking at the ceiling while Rhiannon and I quickly moved apart, he announced, "We should probably think about getting back to Wrightsville Beach."

Reaching out to touch my hand, Rhiannon said, "I wish we didn't have to."

"But we do, much as I hate to say it." Dad walked over to the coffee table and picked up our mugs. The sound of water running came from the kitchen as he rinsed out the mugs and put them in the strainer to dry. When he returned to the living room, Rhiannon and I were standing and ready to go. Once the Jeep was secure back in its shed, we boarded the plane and headed back to that other world.

Twenty-eight

Dusk was falling by the time we landed in Wilmington, and it was dark by the time we dropped Rhiannon off. I got out and walked her to the door. Dad drove on home.

Rhiannon's mother greeted us cheerfully as we entered the house. "The sailors are home from the sea, I see," she said with a bit of a chuckle at her own play on words. Raising an eyebrow, she asked Rhiannon, "Did you have a good time?"

Rhiannon turned and smiled a warm smile at me before answering her mom. "Yes, Momma, it was a perfect weekend."

Mrs. Angevin nodded knowingly. "I'm so glad. I'll get back to the kitchen so you two can say good-bye without your momma's prying eyes."

"Good night, Aunt Cassie," I called to her retreating back.

"Good night, Michael," Mrs. Angevin said over her shoulder, giving me a quick wink and a smile.

As her mom disappeared into the kitchen, Rhiannon put her arms around me. "I wish we were still at River Dream, without your dad."

I brushed my lips lightly against her forehead. "Patience, my love, that day will come."

Rhiannon laid her head against my chest. "It won't come soon enough for me."

"You don't know how good it makes me feel to hear you say that."

Raising her eyes to look into mine, her voice barely above a whisper, Rhiannon declared, "I love you, Michael."

Past the lump in my throat I managed to say, "I love you, Rhiannon."

"See you in the morning," she said as she kissed me.

"I'll be here."

"Good night."

"Good night, I love you."

"I love you."

One final kiss and I really did leave. As I walked home, I noticed Uncle Lind waiting for me in the pier parking lot. I thought, this can't be good.

"Michael, can we take a walk?" he asked.

"Sure, Mr. Angevin," I said. Calling him Uncle Lind right then didn't seem quite right.

He stroked his chin and furrowed his brow before turning and walking toward the beach. I followed him, a little nervous. "Did you kids have a nice weekend?"

He didn't sound upset. I cleared my throat and answered. "Yes, sir, we did."

Nodding and smiling, he resumed his walk. "That's good. I'm glad." Not stopping this time he added, "Michael, I want to tell you something."

Keeping pace with him as he turned to walk up the beach, I replied simply, "Yes, sir." I waited for the hammer to fall.

Mr. Angevin took a deep breath and nodded to himself a few times. He seemed to be trying to decide how to begin.

"You know I was never happy about Rhiannon and Sabrina. I never understood it, and I'm glad Rhiannon has outgrown that phase, if that's the right word. And I'm glad you and Rhiannon are together at last, Michael. I always thought you'd be the one for my little girl."

Our talk wasn't going quite the way I'd expected. "Thank you, sir," I said, wondering where he was going.

Stopping again, Mr. Angevin turned toward me and gave me a long look. The noise from the pier carried to us faintly on the wind, barely loud enough to be heard over the waves crashing on the sand behind me. I looked past Mr. Angevin and noticed the light come on in Rhiannon's window. Shivering a bit from the cool breeze blowing in off the ocean, I looked back at her father.

"Michael, I don't want you to think I'm an unnatural father. A father is not supposed to like the idea of his daughter being with a man, you know what I'm saying?"

My eyes widened as the meaning of his words reached my tired mind. "Yes, sir," I replied, starting to get a little more nervous.

Mr. Angevin laughed a short, soft laugh and looked over my shoulder at the lights on the pier. He bit his lip and looked like he was trying to figure out how to say what he wanted to say next.

"Michael, I've tried to feel upset about you and Rhiannon going away this weekend, but I haven't been able to. I only feel glad she finally let herself see you're the one for her. Does that make me a bad father?"

There were a lot of things I'd expected Mr. Angevin to say to me when he'd invited me on that walk. The idea he was looking to me for reassurance that he was a good father to Rhiannon certainly wasn't one of them. My reply required careful consideration, so I took my time framing my answer. Once I thought I knew what to say, I took a deep breath.

"No, sir. A father whose greatest concern is that his daughter is happy with the man she loves, and that the man loves her back, is a good father, if you ask me."

From the relieved look on his face, he was satisfied with my answer. "Then I'm a good father in your book, Michael, because that's the way I feel. That's how her mother and I both feel." He smiled and put his hand on my shoulder. "Now, do you think you can call me Uncle Lind again? After all, I've known you since before you could walk under my counter without hitting your head."

I could've hugged him but instead shook his offered hand. "Yes, Uncle Lind, I'd like that very much." Uncle Lind suggested I get on home as my parents were probably starting to worry.

When I got home my mother wanted to hear all about the weekend, even though my father had already given her his take on it. She wasn't satisfied with his brief account, so I filled her in on most of what my dad left out. Then I excused myself to go to bed; I was really tired.

My phone started ringing as I closed my door. Thinking it was probably Hans calling to ask how the weekend had gone, I picked it up ready to tell him he would have to wait until the next day to hear all about it. It wasn't Hans.

"Hi, Mike, it's me, Rhiannon," she giggled.

"Well, hi, Rhiannon, long time no see," I said with a smile.

"Fery vunny." It was a phrase we'd coined when we were kids. Her voice became more serious as she asked, "What did you and my dad talk about on the beach?"

Recalling seeing her light come on, I answered her question with a question. "How did you know about that?"

She made an exasperated noise, and I could picture her giving the phone a dirty look. "I saw you guys from my window."

I feigned surprise. "You can see that part of the beach from your window?"

"You know good and well I can, Michael. You and Hans used to scope chicks on the beach from that window," Rhiannon said with a laugh.

"I never did any such thing," I protested, barely getting the words out. "Hans may have scoped for chicks. I was looking for sea shells." Coughing to disguise my laughter, I almost missed her reply.

"Sea shells, right. Now come clean, what did you and Daddy talk about?"

Realizing she seriously wanted to know, and sensing she was a little worried about what might've been said, I was completely honest.

"He wanted me to know he's very happy we're a couple now, and he's glad I'm the guy in love with you and that you're in love with me."

Evidently I did not sound convincing. "What did he really say?" Rhiannon sounded like she was getting a little annoyed.

"If you don't believe me, go ask him," I challenged, more amused than hurt she didn't believe me

"I might just do that; he just came in." She was calling my bluff.

"I'll stay on the phone. You don't even have to hang up."

I could almost see her jaw working as she tried to decide whether or not to call my bluff. "You're not making that up, are you? Wow, my dad, who'd a thunk it."

"I think he likes it we're together."

"Well, I like it we're together, you like it we're together, why shouldn't he like it?"

"Your mom likes it, too," I added.

"She does? How about your parents, do they like it?"

Though I knew she couldn't see it, I shrugged. "No, my parents think you could've done much better."

"You, Michael, are a brat," Rhiannon said as she started to laugh.

"I get that a lot."

"I love you, brat."

"I love you, honey."

We said good-night, and I hung up slowly. I fell asleep and dreamed of Rhiannon at the helm of Riverscape.

Twenty-nine

Spring flew by and suddenly it was time for the prom. I knew I would have to make this prom something special for Rhiannon. Graduation was just over a month away and then I'd be leaving for boot camp almost immediately.

I began wishing I'd scheduled my departure for late August instead of mid June. When I signed the paperwork on my delayed enlistment, I had no reason to want to stay the summer. With Rhiannon and me together, I had all the reason in the world to stay. But changing my departure date was out of the question. That meant making the time we did have so special it would last until we could be together again. So I made my plans and hoped it would be enough.

On prom night I picked Rhiannon up in a white stretch limousine, the kind with a moon roof you can stand up through and watch the world watching you go by. Our first stop was a short way down the island at the Blockade Runner. Our class reserved a whole dining room for prom night dinner. It was a very formal affair.

Rhiannon looked absolutely gorgeous. My heart began to race when I saw her. She wore an emerald green, floor-length, spaghetti-strap, satin gown. Her hair was done in a style I didn't remember ever seeing her wear. While I always preferred her hair down and loose, I had to admit she looked stunning with it up that way. Utilizing a little mom-based espionage, I'd learned what color Rhiannon's gown was going to be and ordered a tuxedo made to match. I'd gone all out with tux, tails, cane, and top hat. I thought I looked rather dashing and debonair. We were a good-looking pair.

Her mom and my mom, both of whom were at Rhiannon's house, had to have pictures, so we didn't leave her house promptly after I arrived. Knowing that was bound to happen, I built it into the schedule.

"Where did you find a tuxedo that matches my gown so well?" Rhiannon asked me once we were in the limo.

Tickled she seemed so pleased, I proudly told her. "I couldn't find one, so I had one made. My mom got the the colors in your gown from your mom and we found a tailor who could match them."

Rhiannon sat back and looked me up and down. "It looks real good on you, Michael."

"Thanks. You look absolutely dazzling. Here, this will add a little more dazzle."

I handed her a small, felt-covered black box. She opened it slowly. "Oh Michael, you didn't."

Unable to keep a self-satisfied smile off my face, I admitted, "Actually, I did."

Rhiannon kept staring into the box. "How did you know about this, Mom again?"

"Mothers talk," I reminded her. "Are you going to put it on?"

"You'll have to put it on for me." She handed me the diamond choker she'd seen at the jeweler's while shopping for her gown. Rhiannon told her mother it would go perfectly with her gown, but there was no way to afford it.

Her mom told my mom about it. My mom told me. I told Dad. Dad went with me, and I bought it. Rhiannon had been dazzling before. Now she positively radiated.

"Michael, I can only accept this because I do know you can afford it. It's beautiful. Thank you, dear Michael. Thank you."

I'd been a bit nervous about giving her the choker, knowing how she felt about my spending money on her, but her reaction was just what I hoped it would be. "Being on you makes it even more beautiful." That may not have made much sense, but she liked hearing it.

She liked even more the looks it got at dinner. "Rhiannon, where did you get that choker? It's gorgeous," April gushed.

"My Michael got it for me." I liked the possessive way she said "My Michael."

"Wow, Michael, do you want an extra girlfriend?" Allie joked.

Rhiannon stood defensively in front of me. "No way, ladies, Michael's all mine," she declared before starting to laugh. Hans laughed, too, but Wes looked a little perturbed. There was nothing I could do about that.

Noticing one of our little circle was missing, I looked around the room. "If you're looking for Beth," Hans guessed, "she's not here."

That piece of news irritated Rhiannon. "No," she said, "why not?"

"Greg, the cheapskate, wouldn't pay for the tickets. He said they'd go to his prom next week, and that ought to be enough for her," explained April.

"I thought they went to his prom last year and were supposed to come here this year," Allie said.

"That's what I thought, too." Rhiannon's contempt for Greg was clear in her voice.

Wes shook his head with disgust. "I never liked that guy."

I didn't say anything. I was disappointed Beth wouldn't be there and kind of mad at Greg, but since there was nothing I could do about it, I decided not to let it get me down.

Our well-dressed serving staff arrived with our salads, and conversation gave way to consumption. The house salad was followed by a light chicken soup that was mostly broth with just a little rice over which a chicken might have been waved. We had pre-ordered our main course dishes. I'd chosen the grilled salmon. The others enjoyed a mix of roasted chicken or beef tips. Rice and a medley of steamed vegetables served as our sides. There were three choices for dessert: chocolate mousse, cheesecake, or a simple dish of vanilla ice cream. After dinner it was time to head to the school for the prom.

Rhiannon pulled me aside as we made our way to the door. "Mike, do you think we could invite the others to join us in the limo? There's enough room."

Knowing how she was probably going to react, I explained cautiously. "Honey, we don't have to. They each have their own. We worked out a deal with the limo company." I pointed to the limos the other couples were getting into.

Rhiannon gave me the suspicious look reserved for when she thought I wasn't telling quite the whole story. "A deal, huh, I bet I know how that worked out. You picked up most of the tab, didn't you?"

"Actually, it's worse than that, I own the livery service. Dad thought it would be a good investment. The guys got a special prom promo price to help generate business for the company."

To my surprise, Rhiannon smiled. "You are something else, Michael Lanier," she said appreciatively and gave me a kiss.

We climbed into our own limo and got settled for the ride. I reached into a small compartment between the forward seats and withdrew a small flower box. "I forgot this before. I hope you like it."

It was a wrist corsage made up of white spray roses, and yellow alstromeria, with a hint of blue heather, arranged on a white lace ribbon with a silver bracelet. Rhiannon put it on and admired it against her gown. "It's beautiful," she said and then kissed me again. "Your forgetfulness is forgiven."

When we arrived at the school we were all impressed by how nicely the prom committee decorated the gym for the event. The theme of our prom was "An Evening in Paradise." The committee decorated the gym to give the impression of a night on a tropical beach, complete with palm trees, strings of little white lights to give the impression of stars, and even a sandy beach leading up to the stage where the King and Queen of the Prom would be crowned.

Each table was spread with a Hawaiian-themed cloth and decorated with a tropical floral arrangement. The tables and chairs were wicker. Real tiki torches had been suggested, but the committee compromised with battery-operated look-alikes spaced all around the dance floor and along the refreshment table. Drinks were served in brightly colored plastic cups with little umbrellas in them.

We were surprised to find Beth there, alone, in her prom gown. "What a great surprise!" Rhiannon exclaimed.

Beth smiled and hugged Rhiannon. "Hey, if Greg didn't want to take me, no law says I can't take myself."

"That's right," Allie said as she gave Beth a hug, too, "phooey on him. You can still have a good time."

"And I intend to," Beth insisted.

We found our table. It was a table for eight. Beth joined us briefly but was called away on some prom committee emergency. I felt guilty that I was glad she left. Darn Greg anyway.

The band started with a song by Billy Joel, "Just the Way You Are," and I asked Rhiannon to dance. We'd been practicing and cut quite a rug. We danced to the next song, too, but then went to the refreshment table for some punch and sat down. Wes and Allie were on the dance floor, but Hans and April were already back at the table.

Hans held up his punch cup in salute to us as we sat down. "You two make quite the attractive pair out there on the floor."

Rhiannon's face lit up at the compliment. "Thank you, Hans."

"You're welcome," Hans replied with a nod that was almost a bow. I kept waiting for the other shoe to drop, but that was all he said. The rest of the night went on about like that: dancing, drinking punch, talking at the table.

Near the end of the night they announced King and Queen of the prom. While the members of the Queen's Court had been announced during the week leading up to the Prom, only select members of the Prom Committee and school staff knew who'd been elected King and Queen.

Rhiannon was selected as a member of the Queen's court, so I got to escort her to the stage to await the announcement of the chosen couple. No surprise to anyone, Kiera Winslow and Deondre Dalton, the head cheerleader and star quarterback, were named King and Queen. While I found it to be a bit cliché, I didn't begrudge them the honor. With all they did around the school, both in and out of sports, they certainly deserved it. Kiera was headed to Duke University on a full academic scholarship, and Deondre had earned an appointment to West Point.

Once the big announcement was made, we stayed on stage to have our picture taken. Much to my disappointment, Rhiannon wouldn't let me wear my top hat. As we returned to our table Hans said, "Michael, come outside with me a moment."

I looked at him quizzically. "Please, Mike," pleaded April, "it's important."

Their obvious anxiety caused me to become concerned. "Do you mind?" I asked Rhiannon.

She looked up from something Allie was saying to her. "You better go, Mike. It's about Beth."

I looked at Hans, who nodded and tilted his head toward the door. "Let's go then."

Hans led me out the side door of the gym. "I don't know if it's anything, but I saw Beth go out this side door and she hasn't come back in yet."

Then we heard the voices. "I don't care if you are on the committee. You had no business coming here without me," we heard Greg say with an angry tone.

"Greg, you're hurting me," Beth cried.

That was all I needed to hear. I handed my jacket to Hans, told him and Wes to watch my back, and closed to contact.

Greg held her by the arms and was shaking her as he leveled his accusation. "You little slut, you came here to see him, didn't you?"

Beth's face showed pain and fear. "No, Greg, I just came because I'm...ow, please let me go."

Greg turned towards me as I walked up on them. "The lady asked you to let her go." My icy tone should've given him a clue to the danger he was in.

"Yeah, so, what're you going to do if I don't?" Greg glanced back over his shoulder, and I noticed he was not alone. Carefully assessing the situation, I counted two of his buddies backing him up. It would be Greg and two meatheads against me. They were hopelessly outnumbered and didn't even know it.

By way of answer to Greg's challenge, I went into overdrive, bypassed him, and took out his two buddies before they even saw it coming. They would be all right when they came to but would hurt for days.

Standing over the sprawled bodies of his unconscious backup, I repeated, "The lady asked you to let her go."

Greg released Beth and raised his hands to his shoulders. "This ain't over, Mike," he warned me.

In a flash I was on him. My knee caught him square in the groin, and as he went down my elbow flashed toward the base of his skull.

"Mike, stop!" Beth yelled. "You'll kill him."

Greg moaned. I knelt down beside him. In a voice only he could hear, I made his options very clear to him. "If you ever go near her again, if you ever lay a hand on her again, I will kill you."

Through his pain he nodded his understanding. I stood up and looked at Beth. "Are you all right?"

Relief flooded her face as she rubbed her bruised arms. "I am now. I was so afraid he'd really hurt me this time."

My receding anger began to rise again. "This time?" I asked through clenched teeth.

Concerned I might finish what I started, Beth quickly added, "He's never actually grabbed me before. Not like that. I was really scared."

Suddenly Greg started to wretch. As he did the school principal arrived on the scene with a sheriff's deputy.

"Does somebody want to tell me what's going on here? Why are those boys on the ground?" Mr. McHale wanted to know.

Beth spoke up at once. "They attacked me. That one," she said pointing to Greg, "used to be my boyfriend."

The deputy noted the three boys struggling to pick themselves up off the ground. "The three of them attacked you?" he asked Beth, sounding not quite convinced.

"Yes, sir. If my friends hadn't come looking for me, I don't know what they might have done to me. Greg said he was going to beat me."

While the deputy considered that, Mr. McHale turned to Hans and Wesley. "Hans, what did you see?"

"We came out for some air, heard Beth scream, and came to help her. The one cradling his privates there had hold of her and was threatening her. The other two appeared to be helping him keep her from getting away. When we came over to help her, they reacted towards us in a way we perceived as a threat."

Mr. McHale raised his eyebrows questioningly, but Hans returned his gaze without wavering. The principal turned to Wes. "Wesley, is that your story?"

"Yes, sir, that's what happened."

Apparently satisfied the two were telling him the truth, Mr. McHale turned to me. "Michael, it's interesting you're the only one of the three of you with his jacket off."

My blood was still up from the encounter, so I was careful with my answer. "I was getting a little hot."

"Yes, I imagine you were," Mr. McHale replied with a wry smile. "Deputy, what is our next step?"

The deputy considered the question for a few seconds before addressing Beth. "Does the young lady wish to press charges against her assailants?"

Beth heaved a tired sigh. "No, I don't think so. I think he'll leave me alone now."

Mr. McHale shook his head and stifled a laugh. "And what makes you think that?" he wondered out loud.

Wes smiled and said, "He just got read the second chapter of the book."

The deputy gave Wes a puzzled look. "Must be an interesting book."

Greg climbed slowly to his feet, and his buddies were sitting up.

"Beth, why don't you see that your rescuers make it back safely to their dates? I think the deputy and I can take it from here. And Michael, stay cool."

Not quite believing he was going to leave it at that, but grateful he was, I very respectfully promised I would.

The deputy and Mr. McHale escorted Greg and his buddies back to their car to see they left campus immediately. Hans, Wes, and I took Beth back inside. The girls were anxious to find out what happened. Beth put it rather succinctly.

"Greg got a little upset when I told him I wanted to break up, and now he's okay with it."

"Somehow," Rhiannon said, looking at me, "I don't think that's the whole story."

"My dear, I don't know what you could possibly mean," I said with all the innocence I could muster.

The last dance, literally the last high school dance for us seniors, was a slow song as might be expected. Beth had managed a little something special for Rhiannon and me. The last song was "Lady" by Styx. It'd sort of become our song.

"Michael, how'd you do it?"

Not knowing if Rhiannon meant the song or how I handled Greg, I asked, "How'd I do what?"

"Our song. How did you get them to end the prom with our song?"

Wishing it was my idea, I admitted, "Honestly, I didn't. I think Beth did it for us."

"Beth, she is something," Rhiannon said. "Do you ever wish…"

Pulling back so that I was looking into Rhiannon's lovely green eyes, I answered, "Never, not for a moment, it was always you."

She smiled and laid her head back on my shoulder. "I'm glad."

Styx played the last strands of "Lady." Our Senior Prom was over. Rhiannon and I held on to each other on the dance floor, reluctant to let go.

"I don't want it to end," Rhiannon said with tears filling her eyes. She was talking about more than just the prom.

Holding her tight, I spoke softly into her ear. "This song is over, but our dance has barely begun."

Smiling she said, "You can be quite the poet, Michael. I love you."

"I love you, Rhiannon," I whispered as I kissed her ever so gently.

"Michael, Rhiannon, it's time to go. The prom is over," Miss Tomlinson said quietly, so as not to break the mood.

"Yes ma'am," we chorused softly. Rhiannon took my arm, and we walked out to our waiting limousine.

This time we were joined by Hans, April, Wes, and Allie. Beth chose to go straight home. It was crowded but cozy.

"Next stop, graduation," said Wes.

"Let's not think about that tonight," April said sadly.

Trying to change the subject, Hans noted, "It was a very nice prom, wasn't it?"

Allie smiled and put her arms around Wesley. "I think it was just what a prom should be."

Wes returned her hug and nodded. Then his expression grew thoughtful. "Except maybe for Beth."

"Beth may have the best prom story of all to tell," Rhiannon said, "rescued by three handsome knights in shining tuxes from the clutches of an evil troll." That got the laugh she hoped it would, and the mood in the limo lightened noticeably.

Our next stop was breakfast at the Pancake House on Oleander Drive. It usually closed at midnight, but arrangements had been made for them to stay open late for prom goers on their way home. We made quite a sight coming in wearing our tuxes and gowns.

A breakfast of Belgian Waffles with whipped cream and blueberry syrup was my choice. I always liked the blueberry. Rhiannon didn't order anything, saying she wasn't hungry, but graciously helped me eat mine. Soon it was time to leave and get everyone home. Rhiannon and I dropped off the others but didn't head straight home ourselves. Instead we went back to the Blockade Runner, where our evening began.

"Michael, what are we doing here?" Rhiannon asked as we exited the limousine. "Why is your car here?" she asked, noticing my GTO in the parking lot.

"Dad dropped the car off so we wouldn't have to walk home." I took her hand and headed into the lobby and beyond. We walked along the boardwalk and out onto the beach.

"Michael, what have you got planned?" Rhiannon asked in a quiet voice.

"Patience, my love, and all your questions shall be answered."

At the edge of the water I reached into my pocket and pulled out a smaller felt-covered black box. By the light from the half-moon, I got down on one knee and took her hand.

"Oh, Michael," Rhiannon said as she realized what I was about to do.

Speaking just loud enough to be heard above the soft breaking of the gentle waves, I began. "Rhiannon, I have loved you since I was old enough to remember. I can't imagine my life without you in it. You're the one I want to spend the rest of my life with. Rhiannon, will you marry me?" I opened the box and held the ring out to her.

"Oh, Michael, my Michael, of course I'll marry you!" Rhiannon cried, taking the ring from the box and slipping it onto her finger. Then she reached down to take my hands and pull me to my feet. "I love you," she said as she moved into my arms. I lowered my head and kissed my fiancé.

Thirty

The last month of senior year went by quickly. Rhiannon and I spent the weekend before graduation in the recently completed house at River Dream, flying up Friday afternoon after school. Friday evening we spent arranging the furniture for the kitchen and master bedroom. It was delivered during the week. I was grateful my dad had been able to go up and meet the delivery truck. There wouldn't be much more furniture in the house for several years.

Graduation took place on June ninth. I managed to make it through my senior year on the Principal's List and graduated with honors. They don't have a fancy Latin name for third in your class, but if they did, that would be me.

We had a big graduation party at Mikey's. It would be the last time most of our class would visit the club as we would all move on to more grown-up pursuits and leave Mikey's to the next class.

Hans, my best friend since forever, had been accepted at North Carolina State in Raleigh. "Mike, what am I going to do up at State without you around to keep me out of trouble?" he asked as we sat around our usual table.

I laughed and punched him playfully on the shoulder. "I guess you'll have to learn to behave yourself, Hans."

"Nein, bro," he protested, pretending to be shocked by the suggestion. "I'll just call you to come post my bail."

Holding my hand to my head like a phone handset, I joked, "Hans, who ist Hans? No sprechen."

"No sprechen zee Irish maybe. But you sprechen zee Deutch just fine, Mike," Hans laughed.

Becoming serious for a moment I put my hand on his shoulder. "My friend, my brother, you know if you really need me, I'll be there."

Hans nodded solemnly. "Same back at you, Mike, anytime, twenty-four hours a day, three hundred sixty-five days a year." He spent the summer before starting college in Germany, visiting relatives and touring his homeland.

Wesley joined the Marines and left for San Diego the day of graduation, so he didn't walk with the class. I don't think Alyssa ever forgave him.

Beth was accepted into the music program at East Carolina University in Greenville on a full scholarship. April was also going to East Carolina, to study nursing. Jill left Wilmington to go live in Asheville with Rick and planned to start classes at Warren Wilson College.

Rhiannon and I planned a long engagement. She'd been accepted at Dartmouth and would be leaving for New Hampshire in the fall. Sitting next to her at Mikey's graduation night, I remembered our discussion about it.

"Dartmouth, in New Hampshire, why would you want to go to school way up there?" I'd asked her when I first learned of it.

She was somewhat defensive in her reply. "It's a very good school, one of the best in the country. I applied last fall before, before you know, and before you and I finally got together. Besides, we've decided not to get married until you get out of the Navy. What difference does it make where I go to school?"

Knowing she had a valid point, I'd started to concede the argument. "It's just that I had in mind you'd be here when I come home on leave."

"So you come to New Hampshire on leave, sweetheart. Listen, Mike, I think this will be good for both of us. I spend four years at Dartmouth while you're in the Navy getting sent who knows where. By the time you get out and come back to UNCW, I'll have graduated and come back here to work. Then we get married and live happily ever after. In the meantime, we see as much of each other as we can. You know they say 'absence makes the heart grow fonder.'"

They also say 'out of sight out of mind,' I thought but didn't say it aloud. "You're right. New Hampshire is a beautiful place. I know my mom likes it up there."

"You are such a reasonable man, Michael," Rhiannon said.

It did seem like a reasonable plan at the time. Rhiannon had known about my plan to join the Navy. It'd been no secret for years. It was also true she'd applied and been accepted before she and I became a couple. What did I expect her to do while I was gone for four years, sit around at home and wait? No, she was right. This plan was a good idea. Rhiannon spent the summer before leaving for Dartmouth working at the pier.

Me, on June 11, 1979, I packed up a few things in an overnight bag, caught a ride with my dad to the airport, and left for the Recruit Training Center in Orlando, Florida. Rhiannon and I said our good-byes the night before. I had a long hot summer in store for me.

My decision to serve in the Navy was not made lightly. My father served in the Navy. All the men in our family in his generation had served in one branch or the other. Both of my grandfathers had served during World War I. I felt I was carrying on something of a family tradition of service.

Part of the decision was also motivated by the sense of patriotism my parents, most vocally my mom, instilled in me. I had been incredibly blessed with a gift I'd done nothing to earn. I felt I owed it to Mr. Justin, who'd been wounded in WWI, to serve my country.

Finally, it meant a chance like no other to learn seamanship. I enlisted to become a Navy small-boat crewman. The Navy Boat Support Units had come into being during Vietnam and were the descendants of the famous PT boats of World War II fame. Boot camp would be followed by advanced training, more training, and more training before finally arriving at my unit. I joined to get lots of small boat experience, and the Navy planned to make sure I got all I could handle.

The one person I hadn't thought much about as I prepared to leave home was my little sister Malori. She'd just turned seven that spring before graduation. What I failed to take into account was how my impending exit from the house was affecting her.

When I got home the Friday afternoon before graduation, I found Malori sitting at the bottom of the stairs to my loft holding a stuffed dolphin I'd given her, crying. "Hey, Mal, what's the matter?"

"Nothing!" she informed me, not looking up and hugging the dolphin closer.

"You're crying for nothing?" I asked in that voice big brothers use when they think their little sisters are acting odd.

Her reply was short, sharp, and to the point. "No."

"Do you want me to get Mom?" I asked, falling back on my standard plan for dealing with Malori's moods.

She closed her eyes and shook her head. "No," she said, softly this time.

Not knowing what to do, but not wanting to leave her alone, I asked if I could sit down.

"Okay," she sadly assented and moved over on the step. I sat down beside her.

Hoping to cheer her up I asked, "Are you glad school's out?"

"No," she said. Then after a short pause. "Well, maybe a little."

I thought I'd discovered the heart of the problem. "Are you sad because you're going to miss your friends?"

Malori sniffed, and the tears started again. "No, they're not going away."

Suddenly it dawned on me. She was sad because I was going away.

"Malori, you know when I'm gone you get to move into the loft," I told her, hoping to help her find a reason to be happy I was leaving.

"Really," she showed the beginnings of a smile, "but where will you sleep when you come home?"

"Mal, I won't be coming back here to live. When I get out of the Navy I'll live in Pamlico County at River Dream."

"Nuh, uh, Michael, Mom won't let you," Malori said. To a seven-year-old kid that trumps all else, Mom said.

It took some effort, but I did not laugh. "Malori, Mom will say it's all right. I'll be a grown-up then."

She looked at me as if trying to picture me as a grown-up. Her eyes squinted and her lips curled. After considering the idea for a moment, she asked, "Will I be grown up when you get back from the Navy?"

I tousled her hair and laughed. "No, kiddo, but you'll practically be a teenager."

"I wish you didn't have to go," Malori said with the start of a sniffle.

The idea of getting my room hadn't done the trick. I thought I knew what might. "I know, but I have to go. Malori, can you do something for me while I'm gone?"

"What?" she asked as she tried not to let her tears show.

"Come out to the dock and I'll show you," I said. Taking her by the hand, I led her down to the dock and out to where Hey 19 was tied up.

"I'm going to need somebody to watch over Hey 19 while I'm gone, someone to take care of her, maybe take her sailing once in a while. Could you do that for me?"

"I'm not big enough to sail your boat all alone, Michael," Malori said with the impenetrable logic of the young.

"Maybe not yet, but Mom and Dad will help you until you are. What do you say, Mal, will you take care of Hey 19 for me?"

Malori looked up at me with the most serious expression I'd ever seen on her little face. "I promise, Michael, I will take very good care of your sailboat," she intoned in a surprisingly adult way.

Now it was my turn to fight back the tears. I realized for the first time how much I was going to miss my little sister. "I know you will squirt. I love you, Malori."

"I love you too, Michael. You're my best brother." I picked her up and she gave me a big hug. I didn't bother to remind her that I was her only brother.

###

About the author

DW Davis graduated from Western New England College with an accounting degree, after a four year hitch in the Army, and is currently working as a middle school math teacher. DW grew up in coastal North Carolina and still resides in the states Coastal Plains region with his lovely wife and two sons. RIVER DREAM is his first novel.

Watch for the next book in the River Dream series:
DREAMS CHANGE

Connect with DW Davis Online:

http://www.riversailorliterary.com
Facebook: http://www.facebook.com/RiverSailorLiterary
Twitter: http://twitter.com/#!/DWDavisRSL
Smashwords: https://www.smashwords.com/profile/view/
riversailorliterary

Made in the USA
Charleston, SC
28 July 2011